MY STOMACH LURCHED. PLEASE GOD, NO. *Claudia* was going to get together with *Luke*? Claudia is so stunning and tall and sultry— basically my opposite. At best, I can pass for normal. If my mouth is closed so you can't see my braces.

"Great!" I lied, fantasizing fondly about shoving my ruler up her nose.

"Do you think Luke will let me see his DVD collection?" Claudia continued loudly to Poppy. I saw with horror that Claudia was writing *C loves L* in pen on her desk. "I always wanted to be a film director when I was little."

I wanted to look at Poppy again but knew I would give myself away by looking really hurt. How could she allow this to happen? I know I tried to stop her making embarrassing comments about me and Luke, but she knew how much I liked him! Instead I occupied myself by laughing loudly at something Sasha had said. Which only alarmed Sasha, as she'd been asking Charlotte if there was an accent in *"recevoir."*

Does Snogging Count as Exercise?

HELEN SALTER

Does Snogging Count as Exercise?

SIMON PULSE
NEW YORK   LONDON   TORONTO   SYDNEY

SIMON PULSE

An imprint of Simon & Schuster

Children's Publishing Division

1230 Avenue of the Americas, New York, NY 10020

Copyright © 2005 by Helen Salter

Originally published in Great Britain in 2005 by Piccadilly Press, Ltd.

Published by arrangement with Piccadilly Press, Ltd.

All rights reserved, including the right of reproduction in whole or in part in any form.

SIMON PULSE and colophon are registered trademarks of Simon & Schuster, Inc.

Designed by Karin Paprocki

The text of this book was set in Bembo Std.

Manufactured in the United States of America

First Simon Pulse edition November 2007

2 4 6 8 10 9 7 5 3 1

Library of Congress Control Number 2006940712

ISBN-13: 978-1-4169-3801-9

ISBN-10: 1-4169-3801-X

This book is for all my friends,
particularly Faye, Rachel, Kate, Rebecca,
Charlie, and Joëlle—gorgeous, talented,
and inspirational, one and all

ACKNOWLEDGMENTS

THANKS ARE DUE TO THE WHOLE TEAM AT Piccadilly, especially Brenda, Yasemin, and Melissa for their support, guidance, and vision. I'd also like to say thanks to Brian Keaney at the Literary Consultancy for his enthusiasm, and to thank my family and boyfriend for still being nice even while I lay supine on my sofa complaining dramatically of extreme stress. I should also acknowledge Jasmine and the dearly departed Smudge for helpful paw prints on the manuscript and gifts of worms and leaves (leaves?!) from the garden. The final debt of gratitude is to my school friends who filled up all those rough books with notes and kept me awake during math lessons—it's amazing we got GCSEs, etc., and went on to be such fine upstanding citizens.

My Family and Other Animals

NINETY PERCENT OF PEOPLE IN YEAR NINE
have already snogged somebody!" yelled Poppy
into the phone. Clearly a survey in one of her
magazines had confirmed that we were trailing hap-
hazardly behind all normal people on the planet.

I sat in the hall listening to Poppy on the landline
and I wondered if cool stuff ever happened in real life,
or just in American high school films. You know what
I mean. The kind of things that you fantasize about
during double math:

HOLLY STOCKWELL'S
FAVORITE FANTASIES

1. I arrive at the school gate on the back of a motorbike driven by Luke. He screeches to a halt and I

slip gracefully off the bike, shaking my hair out of my crash helmet (gorgeous, shiny, blond, or, if I am feeling particularly imaginative, all three).

2. Instead of walking past my house as he usually does, Luke runs toward it in slow motion, climbs up the porch to my window, like in *Romeo and Juliet*, and presents me with a rose he is holding between his teeth.

3. I am in a math class (no, that's not it—there's more) when Luke bursts in holding a huge bunch of flowers for me. Optional extended scene: He then takes me outside and snogs me in the playground—since witnessing such unbridled passion would probably give Mrs. Craignish a heart attack.

Unfortunately, I had never even spoken to a boy I fancied, let alone had one deliver flowers to my desk. Well, okay, I'd spoken to Luke once when he answered the door at Poppy's house. Our entire conversation went like this:

Me: Oh—hi!

Luke (hurriedly): I'll get Poppy. *(Runs away)*

 2

While Poppy went on about our romantic ineptitude, I squished the receiver against my ear in case Ivy or—God forbid—Mum could hear her. Poppy didn't have the wildest life either, but she did have the advantages of unlimited mobile phone calls, Luke as an older brother, and, most importantly, chilled-out parents. (My parents? I still have to hide my copy of *Forever* by Judy Blume, in case it spontaneously falls open at the rude pages.)

"You almost-snogged Yves," I whispered. (Highlight of Poppy's family holiday last summer: Random French boy put his arm round her on the beach and leaned toward her but then his dad turned up.)

"That doesn't count."

"Well, maybe we just haven't had as much opportunity because we go to an all-girls school," I said to reassure us both, while trying to untwiddle the phone cord. The landline phone in my house is not even a cordless one you can take into your room. It just sits there in the downstairs hall and you have to sit there with it, at risk from eavesdropping mothers.

"What . . ." Poppy slowed down. "Like, if there were boys, you'd get to do snogging in school?"

"Yeah, French kissing. For GCSE."

God, I thought—if there was some kind of course in how to deal with boys, I would definitely join up (and I'd enjoy the practicals). I'd always be putting my hand up to ask questions. How are you supposed to practice talking to boys when you don't know any? What do you say to make them like you?

Poppy snorted. "Miss Rustford would go, 'Now, girls, gently moisten your lips . . .'"

"Urrrgghhh!"

Poppy wisely changed the subject. "Anyway, I was calling to say my parents can't drive us to the youth club tonight."

At which point all my plans for the entire year— well, tonight—abruptly went WHOOSH out of the window. Did her parents not realize that even though the youth club was, admittedly, a bit rubbish, the car ride provided a chance of sitting by Luke in the backseat? And maybe bumping knees when going round tight corners?

"No Jez, then!" I said, stoically ignoring my own pain (fourteen-year-olds should not be so pathetic and dependent on knee-bumping).

"Oh Jez . . ." There was a crashing noise indicating that Poppy had yet again swooned and dropped her mobile at the mention of his name. Poppy had known and fancied Jez for ages, to the point where they were such good mates that Poppy had no idea if he fancied her and didn't want to risk messing things up by finding out—although I was sure I'd seen him look lingeringly at her across the table-football table, which was a Good Sign. (Note: Jez is very nice in a sandy-haired, posh sort of way, but nowhere near as gorgeous as Luke. Although of course I wouldn't tell Poppy that.)

"Is Luke bothered that we can't go?" I asked, hoping Poppy would say, "Holly, he's devastated he won't be seeing you. He's upstairs right now crying his eyes out."

But Poppy just returned to her handset *après-swoon* and said, "No—he's going to the cinema with Craig instead. He didn't invite me. As if he's so cool just because he's sixteen. All he ever does is hang out with Craig or talk about old Bond films, and rubbish film directors. Or something else that's dull!"

I kept quiet. Old Bond films are clearly brilliant. And it is cool that Luke wants to direct films one day. (Though I think he should star in them instead. He's got this gorgeous, dark curly hair and these green eyes . . . mmm.)

"I was thinking, right, about tonight—," began Poppy, when Dad and my little brother, Jamie, suddenly burst in through the front door.

"I got them!" yelled Jamie, proudly brandishing a sports shop bag. Ugh. Okay, he couldn't help being only eleven, but Mum and my big sister, Ivy, should have known better. They emerged from the living room and, bafflingly, started cooing over Jamie's new trainers.

"Sshh!" I said, but unfortunately this just made them realize I was a) there, and b) on the phone. "Sorry, Plop—not you," I added hastily into the phone.

"Why don't you just go and see Poppy?" interrupted Dad. "Honestly. You've just spent all week together at school. She's only a short walk up the road!"

Sometimes I wonder if I was actually switched at birth, and if somewhere else in South London there is a book-loving, academic family whose tracksuit-wearing, racquet-wielding daughter is always nagging *them* to get some fresh air.

"You know, get some fresh air?" said Dad.

See what I mean? I looked at Mum, who had sat down on the stairs to put laces into Jamie's trainers, and knew that if I carried on talking, she'd blatantly listen in anyway. I don't even think she realizes there's anything wrong with eavesdropping on me. She's simply oblivious to my privacy rights. I'm surprised she doesn't disguise herself as a bit of furniture and sit in the hall all day for surveillance purposes.

"Hang on," I told Poppy resignedly. "I'll come over."

WHEN I WENT ROUND TO POPPY'S, LUKE was heading out to meet Craig and on the way past me his coat brushed my elbow! For a micromillisecond at least we were fused, as one, in the universe! Not bad going considering it was only mid-January. Poppy noticed and opened her mouth to make a comment, but I successfully silenced her with a glare. God, Poppy could be so embarrassing, if I let her. I hadn't told her for ages that I fancied Luke, because the potential for cringeworthy comments was so great.

Besides, I had even more ambitious plans for the year ahead:

HOLLY STOCKWELL'S NEW YEAR'S RESOLUTIONS

1. Snog someone. (A gorgeous boy, I mean—e.g. Luke. Not just anyone. Not the bus driver.)

2. Go on one of those group holidays with Poppy, without parents, in order to possibly achieve No. 1 on a beach at sunset.
3. Avoid PE (no way can I follow Mum's advice to just enjoy taking part and not get in a blind panic about it).
4. Get better-looking, e.g. get smaller bottom, get rid of braces, and somehow transform tangled hair into Pantene-style gorgeousness. (Tangled hair no good for seduction—how will boys run their fingers through it?)
5. Stop buying *CosmoGIRL!*, as I'll just end up wanting glittery lip gloss due to glittery lip gloss feature but will have spent all my money on the magazine.
6. Improve social life by going out to more good parties.
7. Okay, go to any parties.

The first two were joint with Poppy, so that we could spur each other on. My main resolution was the Luke-snog. Poppy had almost-kissed Yves, so I needed to catch up.

Poppy and I sat in her room and ate Whoppers while she checked her moles in her bedroom mirror.

Ever since I've known Poppy she has been a total hypochondriac. Every time she gets a cramp in her foot she thinks it's deep vein thrombosis and her leg is going to fall off.

"Sorry about just now on the phone," I told her. "Jamie finally bought these new trainers with his Christmas money. He's been deciding which ones to get for weeks."

"Has your mum forgiven you yet for what you did with yours?"

"No, not really." Honestly, you would have thought Christmas money was yours to do what you liked with, but mine had been accompanied by lots of hints from Mum and Dad about getting some sensible hiking boots, prompted by the mysterious incident where I had left my previous pair on a bus. They weren't too pleased when I spent it all on a novel and some pay-as-you-go mobile phone credit, which was already gone.

"I was going to say on the phone—tonight, we could call Jez and go out in town instead?" said Poppy hopefully.

"I'd love to," I said from my usual spot by the window, watching Poppy twist and turn trying to see the back of her shoulder. "But can you imagine what my mum would say? *Town in the evening?* She'd be convinced we'd get lost."

"Or mugged," Poppy added, who was used to my mum.

"Or, worse—Jez would lead us astray."

"Mmm." Poppy frowned into the mirror. She seemed a bit frustrated by my inability to go out—which was a bit rich, considering that she wouldn't actually dare ask Jez out in a million years. Not to mention that this time it was her parents who were inadvertently preventing us from seeing him, due to their refusal to take us to the youth club. Maybe all parents are secretly in cahoots and take turns thwarting boy-related plans?

"Don't you think it's horrid having so many moles?" said Poppy, squinting critically at herself in the mirror.

"No," I said automatically. "They're only little freckles!"

"I've got really bad skin."

"No, you haven't."

"And my hair is falling out. I'm going bald!"

"You are not! It's curly, that's all. It just looks like a lot when one comes out."

"Oh my God. This is a totally new mole. That's not good, is it? Look!"

"That's a bit of Whopper."

"Hmm," said Poppy, looking slightly pacified. Then she added, "But I really wish we could go out and do something cool."

She knew I'd love more than anything to have a mammoth night out, but what could we do? Being fourteen is not like it is in films and books and stuff, where the characters spend all their time dancing at illicit parties, sneaking into rock concerts, winning *Pop Idol*–type contests, etc. There is clearly a magic formula required in order to have cool stuff happen to you:

Cool Stuff Guaranteed if . . .

- you're a Californian.
- you're an identical twin.
- you're named Tori or Sandi or similar.
- you have a secret talent for something, e.g. dancing, with which to hugely impress some gorgeous boy.
- your parents are going away for the weekend.

No Cool Stuff Imminent if . . .

- you're from South London.
- you're the middle child of three.
- you're named Holly as a hilarious comedy follow-up to older sister Ivy.
- you're forced to do PE (with no secret talent for it).
- your parents are showing no signs of leaving you alone in the house, ever.

My mum let me out for the Friday night youth club, because Poppy's parents knew the organizers and drove us safely there and back, but most other bids for freedom involved a lengthy Boy-Meeting Risk Assessment—as if I was ten, not fourteen! She genuinely thinks I am too young for "such things." My mum is convinced that all boys are Very Dangerous and permanently prowling around for fourteen-year-old girls to make pregnant and/or addicted to cigarettes. I think she must get such ideas from reading the papers, because the highlight of Poppy's and my weekend is usually seeing who can fit the most marshmallows in her mouth at once.

"Do you want to come over this weekend?" Poppy asked as I was playing with Mouse. (Poppy had not been the most imaginative twelve-year-old when it came to the pet-naming department.)

I rolled my eyes. "I can't. My family's doing a sponsored Fun Run. Ivy's come back specially from uni for the weekend. I've got to go along."

Poppy giggled for a long time, then said, "Oh my God, Holly—they're not still hoping you'll get inspired?"

"Apparently. Ugh. They're all so . . . *active*. It's

exhausting just watching them." I tried to laugh. I suppose it was funny, looking at it objectively. I feel much more at home with my friends than with my family. My friends don't care if I prefer books and films to volleyball, but it is a big deal in my family!

"So don't go."

"It's not that easy. They are all so into it! It's easier just to go with the flow."

"I guess they're just . . . very enthusiastic," said Poppy kindly, whose parents are nice and normal and don't own matching tracksuits.

"I'll go, but I'm not joining in!"

"You know, Holly, most people rebel against their parents by dyeing their hair blue or doing Class-A drugs. You rebel by sitting in your mum's car with a book."

"Honestly," I said, sighing. "Since when did the words 'fun' and 'run' belong together in the same sentence? I hate running."

"You ran for that bus last week."

"Only because I thought Luke was on it."

A Winter's Tale

SUNDAYS SHOULD BE BANNED. THEY always just involve doing homework in a panic at the last minute, followed by my friend Sasha phoning me for the answers, endearingly confident that I will know everything. I do try to tell her that I am no genius, but sometimes it is indeed best to go through stuff with her, like back at the end of the Christmas holidays when she got her subjects tangled up. ("You know that essay we were supposed to write about euthanasia? I can't find it on the map!")

The only thing that made that particular Sunday worthwhile was Luke walking past en route to the newsagent's. (Luke walking past is a big event in South London. No, really, it is. Jamie got excited the other day when he saw a cloud shaped like a dog.) Being in the rubbish boxroom at the front of the house did have one advantage: It allowed me to Luke-watch subtly out of the window. Also, my bedroom was above the porch, which could theoretically provide secret access for fit boys. Of course, this has never actually happened.

Saturday was enlivened by the Fun Run, of course, during which I followed my usual plan:

RULES FOR ATTENDANCE OF ANOTHER RIDICULOUS SPORTING EVENT (A.R.S.E. FOR SHORT)

1. Outline logical reasons why I should stay in the car (seal belt stuck, risk of rain, etc.).
2. Proceed reluctantly to site of sporting activity, carrying book and mobile phone.
3. Locate most comfortable spot on the sidelines and ignore interruptions by crazed mother holding spare racquet/pedometer/other baffling bit of sports paraphernalia in an attempt to persuade me to join in.
4. Remind mother that sadly I have brought nothing practical to wear.
5. Sit on sidelines while family hits balls/runs long distances/combination of the two.

Thank God for text messages—I could merrily exchange texts with Poppy for hours (or sometimes Sasha, but she was often hanging out with her friends in the park near her house, whereas I could rely on Poppy's social life to be just as limited as mine). It was much easier to text friends during ARSEs than it was to argue that I should stay at home. It kept me occupied quite happily until it was time to be driven back home (surrounded by other people's medals and muddy shoes).

Mum looked a bit gutted after the Fun Run when Ivy had to get the train back up to uni. Ivy and Mum used to do loads of sporty stuff together before Ivy went to uni. Although, Ivy still fueled all Mum's conversations with her friends at the badminton club. ("Ivy's enjoying the first year at uni! Yes . . . sports science. So she can be a coach!") Huh. Mum never mentioned the fact that Ivy totally messed up her A-levels. Although I get good grades at school, as a non-ball-catcher I am subtly, but firmly, considered a second-class citizen.

Ivy's sportiness had even won her the fight for the newly converted loft room! She's got a huge rowing machine and exercise bike, but was only supposed to have the room until she went to uni. During the upheaval I had stupidly agreed to a temporary room swap with Jamie as his dartboard and punchbag were clogging up the living room. But now Ivy had been at uni since September and I was still in the boxroom! I knew if I raised it with Mum, she would say that Ivy would be back for holidays and stuff. I didn't want to make a fuss. And I definitely didn't want to be the person who emphasised that Ivy was more or less gone for good. So there I was in the smallest room known to man, with Jamie's old cabin bed and wonky footballers crayoned on the wall.

ACTUALLY, MAYBE PEOPLE ARE TOO HARSH on Sundays. At least Sunday boredom is of your own making, not forced down your throat like on a rainy Monday at school. Perhaps the government should just make England go straight from Saturday to Tuesday? All the stuff that didn't get done on Mondays could be given to unemployed people and then everyone would be happy.

At breakfast on Monday, Jamie was hoping for it to snow so school could be canceled, which was not a bad thought. After all, rain is just wet and boring, whereas the snow idea gave me a whole new range of

Luke fantasies: Luke throwing snowballs, putting his arm around me while walking through the snow, etc. (It is amazing that snow and rain are actually the same molecules, just in different moods.)

I had exchanged weekend gossip (none) with Sasha, Charlotte, Bethan, and the rest of the gang by nine a.m., and it was downhill from there. Our form teacher Miss Rustford told us delightedly in registration that we would continue with our swimming lessons in spring term. Ugh. Surely school should be a nice, warm, fuzzy refuge from enforced physical exercise?

REASONS PE SHOULD CLEARLY BE BANNED

1. Who needs the whole dread-of-getting-picked-last thing when teams are chosen?
2. Competitive situations are really scary.
3. PE either makes you wet and cold and smell of chlorine (swimming) or sweaty (everything else).

Oh, and our PE teacher, Mrs. Mastiff, always makes us wear those stupid swimming caps. Mine was a birthday present from Mum, but ever since Jamie and his best friend, Evil Liam, had punched holes in it with a hole puncher, my hair kept getting wet, even though I had quietly tried to mend it with Dad's bicycle puncture repair kit.

Usually Poppy and I exchanged notes in registration, finishing off whatever conversation we'd begun on the bus, but she'd forgotten her rough book. So, while Miss Rustford went on about swimming, I read the latest graffiti written on the desks. One inscription read: *I love Julian!* Julian had been Claudia Sheringham's latest boyfriend, until he was dumped for not spending enough money on her Christmas present. Being both confident and gorgeous (in a dark-haired, Mediterranean sort of way), Claudia was the subject of the most exotic rumors in Year Nine. Sasha once told me that Claudia had snogged *five* boys at a party, and didn't even know all their names! That is what you can do if you hang around with the girls in Year Ten and your Italian mum just happens to be a TV actress. It seemed clear to me that all the girls who had failed to snog someone by the age of fourteen probably lived in the same area as Claudia, who was Hoovering up all the boys, leaving no chance for people with an overprotective mother, fixed braces, and boring light brown hair.

Suddenly, Miss Rustford changed the subject from

bad to worse. She stopped going on about swimming and instead handed out another letter about the Year Nine and Ten skiing trip to the French Alps! I had been roped into going by the powers that be. First Poppy wanted me to go because it was her birthday on the last day and she said she needed someone to talk to in hospital if she broke her leg. Then Mum found the letter in my room while hanging up my school shirts and started going on about fresh alpine air. I suggested to Mum that she pay for Sasha instead of me, since Sasha actually wanted to go and her parents couldn't afford it, but apparently that wasn't an option. My parents aren't exactly loaded (judging by the way my pocket money only pays for about ten percent of the necessary mobile phone credit), so, clearly, behind all their enthusiasm was the hope that I'd come back transformed into a fitness fanatic. (I could just imagine the conversation around the swingball: "Let's send her skiing!" "Brilliant, then she'll happily wear horrid fleecy tracksuits and join us for ten-mile hikes in the rain!")

Okay, I do feel bad that when Mum was a teenager she was supposed to become a brilliant sportswoman, before her knee injury and all that, but I'm just not good at sports! I said I'd go, so as not to upset her, but quietly wondered if there was any way to avoid the actual skiing. . . .

THINGS TO DO IN THE FRENCH ALPS THAT DON'T INVOLVE HURTLING DOWN A MOUNTAIN

1. Have flattering photos taken in sunglasses with a beautiful mountainous backdrop.
2. Sit in cafés drinking hot chocolate.
3. Warm toes on furry white rug in front of roaring log fire.
4. Snog fit local French boys.

Miss Rustford looked around the class. "Does anyone have any questions about the trip?"

"When can we sort out the room sharing?" I asked. One good thing about the skiing trip was that being away with friends would be fun.

Miss Rustford let out a Very Big Sigh. She is one of the grumpiest people on the planet. It was really annoying having her as our French teacher as well as our form teacher.

"Ivy—I mean, Holly—the skiing is the main concern. We can organize rooms later."

Why were teachers *still* calling me Ivy? Okay, we both have light brown hair and a similar physique (well, we're both on the short side and fairly slim—though my bottom is bigger). But Ivy left the sixth form last year! Moreover, she is Athletic Genius Girl, while I am Academic-Scholarship Girl (I think I won the pity vote after they misguidedly trialed me for the annual Sports Scholarship).

Poppy, who was sitting next to me, looked unsatisfied. "What about . . . amenities?"

"Amenities?" asked Miss Rustford.

"You know, like a sweet shop."

"And a boys school," said Claudia Sheringham loudly. Poppy laughed.

Miss Rustford's frown didn't even flicker!

I THINK THAT MY ONLY ACHIEVEMENT THE whole of Monday was creating a Who-Likes-Who chart in the back of my rough book during math. You just put lots of circles on a page and write the names of everyone you know in them (your friends, that is, not your next-door neighbor). Then you join them up:

WHO-LIKES-WHO CHART

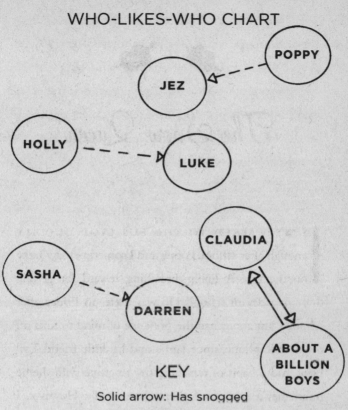

KEY

Solid arrow: Has snogged

Broken arrow: Fancying is in progress

but nothing has happened yet

Claudia was on there merely to add interest. It was probably a bad move. Judging by what I had heard, I risked using up all my pens trying to accurately document her love life.

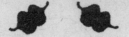

The Snow Queen

IF WE WALKED TO THE BUS STOP QUICKLY enough after school, Poppy and I sometimes saw Luke on the bus! A living, breathing reward for getting through a day of school! He was there on Friday after school. I just about had the presence of mind to turn off my mobile phone, since Jamie and his little friend, Evil Liam, had a habit of replacing my ringtone with theme tunes they'd composed themselves—badly. However, I couldn't alter the fact that, as usual, I was wearing the Ultimate Anti-Boy Apparel (hideous Burlington Girls' purple duffel coat and purple-and-gray-striped school scarf). On this occasion it was compounded by Poppy leading the way and sitting down a few rows in front of Luke, even though there were empty seats parallel to him! A total disaster, for two reasons: First, the daily bus journey was specifically for looking at Luke (yum—that amazing, infectious grin, which always gave you a sudden, irresistible urge to hug him; I always found it best to hold on to the nearest fixed object to make sure I didn't). Second, I was having a firework-hair day (exploding in all different directions, potentially hazardous to others, should be restricted to once a year on a dark November night). I tried casually putting my hand up behind my head to cover it up, but Poppy just looked at me oddly and muttered under her breath, "What are you doing?" so I put my hand down and replied, "Just making sure my head doesn't fall off."

But I couldn't stop thinking about how Luke could see the back of my head, in full-on gruesomeness, so I turned to stare out of the window instead. I even remembered to keep my mouth closed in case he was blinded by the reflection of my braces in the bus window. So that was all fine until I realized Luke would be getting a PROFILE of my head, which was even worse, because then he'd think, "Blimey, I've never seen hamster cheeks like that!" In the end I rummaged in my bag for the full length of the journey, pretending to look for lip balm.

Having a head is such a liability sometimes.

P LOP, IMAGINE IF WE GOT SNOWED IN," I said later that evening. We were in the small lobby of the youth club, putting on our coats to go home. We had finally made it to see Jez. Poppy's parents were a bit worried that the roads would be icy, but Poppy convinced them it would be fine. I don't know how she does it! Maybe everyone has been on a Parent Management course except me?

"Getting snowed in would be really boring!" said Poppy.

"No, it would be good. We could light a fire to keep warm—you know, like in disaster movies."

Poppy's coat fell off its peg and her voice went muffled as she bent to pick it up. "God, you're as bad as Luke, going on about films."

I was about to say something back, when Luke walked in. "What's this?" he said, evidently having heard his name.

I looked at him, opened my mouth, and—and stopped. What should I say? It was definitely good timing to say something. It just needed to be devastatingly funny and original. I paused to consider it, when an unfamiliar beeping noise broke the silence.

"What's that?" said Luke, looking confused.

"I don't know." This came out a bit whispery for some reason. Great. I cleared my throat.

He stood looking around, trying to locate the sound.

"It's someone's phone. What tune is that?"

"It's *Postman Pat*," interrupted Poppy, helpfully pulling my phone out of my coat pocket!

I looked down wildly. Jamie. I knew it! I turned my phone off and quickly put it away, not wanting Luke to see how embarrassingly old it was.

"Er, what made you choose that tune?" said Luke, directly to me. Directly to me! Seven whole words! (If "er" counts as a word, which I think it does.)

I was saved from actually having to reply by Mr. and Mrs. Taylor phoning Poppy to say they'd arrived to collect us. On the way to the car I tried a walking-fast maneuver so that I could sit next to Luke in the back seat (not to be confused with a walking-fart maneuver, something entirely different perfected by Evil Liam). However, when I got in, Luke edged up really close against the window and then just stared the other way! It was so unfair. Poppy and Jez had talked properly for at least five minutes. How does she manage it? I was hopeful at one point when the car skidded a bit on some ice that Luke and I would get to bump knees, but Mr. Taylor swiftly recovered full control of the vehicle.

HOW COOL. LITERALLY. IT SNOWED ON

Saturday night! Jamie was delighted. People on the news were saying that the country was in chaos! Even better, Luke and I went to Kestrel Hill together and skidded down on bin liners! Being with him was so romantic.

Well . . . Poppy was there too.

Well . . . okay, it was too icy for Luke to go round to Craig's, so he was actually trapped with us.

But he chucked loads of snowballs and three hit me really hard! It was like a metaphor for Cupid's arrow! Although more painful. At one point Poppy caught me looking wistfully at Luke and raised her eyebrows teasingly. "Are you okay there, Holly?"

"Shut up!" I said to her, panicked. God, she can be so embarrassing sometimes.

"What?" Luke looked up from packing a snowball.

"Nothing," I said hurriedly, and looked away. But when I looked back he wasn't looking at me anymore.

At one point as the sun was setting, Luke and I

raced down the hill on bin liners and landed in a tangled heap! I pretended to be slightly more dazed than I really was, in order to prolong the tangled-heapiness of the situation, but unfortunately he got up really quickly and threw some snowballs at Poppy.

Afterward, Poppy was convinced she'd caught pneumonia, so I made her a hot chocolate at my house, and she accidentally left behind Luke's scarf that she had borrowed! It smelled lovely, like aftershave. I hoped she would forget it permanently, so it could stay in its rightful home under my pillow.

LIST OF ACHIEVEMENTS SO FAR THIS YEAR

1. Items of Luke's clothing I still have in my possession—**1**
2. Tangled heaps landed in with Luke—**1** (hurrah!)

Meanwhile, I wrote Luke a letter telling him how much I liked him. Of course, I never actually send them! I'm not mad. I just folded it inside my copy of *Anne of Green Gables*, where Mum would never look.

Bonjour Tristesse

ZUT ALORS, AS MARIE-CLAUDE FROM OUR French textbook would say. We had to go to school the following Monday. Just because the snow melted! Jamie was gutted.

First thing we had math and instead of enjoying the snow like all normal people, Mrs. Craignish had used her weekend to mark the previous week's spontaneous test! I only got eight out of ten, which was a bit rubbish for me, but then again Sasha only got four. (Not that I am a really horrible person who is reassured by the failures of their friends.)

At lunchtime Bethan looked at the pictures on Poppy's phone, and a close-up photo of Luke went all round our gang in about five minutes flat! Bethan is permanently gathering and sharing snippets of news, especially any relating to fit boys.

"Have you all seen this picture of Poppy's brother?" she asked everyone in earshot, passing Poppy's phone to Sasha. "He's *gorgeous*!"

Claudia was walking past with Cool Tanya from Year Ten. "Who's this?" she asked, leaning over and lightly plucking the phone from Sasha's hand, at which Sasha glowered silently. Sasha thinks Claudia is a stuck-up cow and often launches into a true Sasha-style rant about her. ("The way she goes on about her house in Lansdowne, just because it's a posh area! And her mum's stupid soap opera! My mate Adèle watches it when she bunks off school and she says it's rubbish!")

"Poppy's brother. Fit or what?" said Charlotte succinctly, looking over Claudia's shoulder. Bethan nodded. I was delighted by this affirmation from the rest of our class. Well, not the *whole* class, but Charlotte and Bethan's opinion counted. I occasionally sat next to them if Poppy was off school with some imaginary illness and Sasha was bunking off with Adèle.

"Not bad!" said Claudia. Even Cool Tanya nodded! Claudia handed Poppy's phone back to her, smiling. The warm glow of fame by association was intoxicating. No one else got to see Luke almost every day and had landed in a tangled heap with him!

By half-past history I was feeling spurred on enough by my close connections to organize something involving Luke—anything—for the weekend. Well, almost. It was all in my head. Also, Mum would have a heart attack. But in Fantasy World, Poppy and I could arrange to meet Luke and some friends of his in town. It would be almost like a date! Poppy could take pictures on her phone and everyone would see me with Luke!

In the back of my rough book I wrote a list of hurdles I would need to overcome in order to achieve the above, which had the added advantage of making me look really busy and productive in the lesson:

1. Get Poppy to invite Jez.
2. Phone Luke (ignoring obvious additional hurdle of Mum listening in while I talk on landline).
3. Possibly clarify who I am to Luke.
4. Present compelling reasons as to why Luke would want to agree to the above, along with his friends, whom I've never met.

I was going to talk to Poppy in French about my plan (in the French lesson, that is, not *in French*) but

Claudia sat next to her, even though she knew that was my seat! Not that I was bothered by it. I was not bothered at all.

D ARREN FLICKED A BIT OF GUM AT ME last night!" Sasha declared into the phone later. "Which means he totally fancies me."

"Okay," I said doubtfully. I rely on Sasha for boy knowledge, but was that definitely a sign of undying love? Initially Sasha had called needing the answers to the English comprehension before going out to Darren's house. I had managed to get hold of the landline from Dad while he was ponderously reciting our phone number. (Why can't he ever just say hello like a normal human being?) Then Sasha updated me on her eventful love life. She is so lucky—she is always out getting a GCSE in Flirting with her mates, who are mostly boys. So there she is, gathering compliments on her latest elaborate hair extensions or gorgeous beaded plaits that took her auntie in the salon six hours to do, while I am in my bedroom with Poppy getting her to say "BOY!" really loudly to see if there is a listening device anywhere that will prompt my mum to burst through the door in a blind panic.

"Then," Sasha continued blithely, "he put his arm around me and said he'd always fancied curvy girls!"

"Ah." I thought Sasha might be underwhelmed by the dramatic developments in my own love life (secret possession of Luke's scarf and landing in tangled heap), so instead I told her about Poppy and Jez at the youth club. "They chatted for a bit then Jez stole Poppy's bus pass so he could look at the photo!"

"A well-known flirtation tactic," judged Sasha.

SASHA'S LIST OF DEFINITE FLIRTING SIGNALS

1. Wanting to see someone's bus pass photo.
2. Talking about the best children's TV programs from when you were little.
3. Going on about things you have in common (e.g. both having brown eyes, the letter "e" in your names, the ability to breathe, etc.).

Sasha continued. "Did Poppy steal Jez's bus pass right back so they were forced to have a bit of a tussle?"

"No. Poppy ignored that he'd taken it and just started chatting about Jez's new trainers."

"Does she definitely fancy him?"

Ha!

"Definitely," I said, laughing a bit. "Poppy talks about Jez all the time." You could tell Sasha and Poppy don't really hang out together that much. It's not that they don't like each other, it's just that they don't really know each other. Sasha is my friend from primary school and because she lives quite far away, even I don't see her outside school all that often.

"Then you two are as bad as each other!" said Sasha.

"No—it's totally different from me and Luke. Poppy actually talks to Jez for hours. It's really impressive. But they're already really good mates—she's worried about messing it up."

"Stuck in the Friend Zone," said Sasha wisely, although I don't think she's dipped a toe in the Friend Zone in her life. "You should get them together!"

I snorted. "I wouldn't be any help."

"Why not?"

Sasha didn't understand; boys were just a different species. I didn't even know any to practice talking to, apart from Jamie and Evil Liam, who didn't count. How could I help Poppy and Jez when I couldn't even chat to Luke without clamming up? And even if I did have

Luke climbing up my porch, Mum would still be there, checking my every move!

When I got off the phone, Mum emerged from the living room and said nosily, "Sasha asking you for help with her homework again?"

Mum hasn't approved of Sasha ever since a small cheating incident during last year's exams, where Sasha wrote the answers on a bit of paper she pinned inside her skirt, which I thought was quite inventive. But Sasha is fab. Poppy is my best friend, but I've known Sasha for longer. We first met, aged five, when she threw a red plastic brick at our teacher. (It's just as well Mum doesn't know about that.)

I glared at Mum and went upstairs.

B Y THE FOLLOWING EVENING TWO PROB-lems had emerged. First, the smell of Luke's aftershave on his scarf had completely disappeared! I should have taken smaller sniffs. I thought about it scientifically and tried breathing back out through my nose so the molecules would go back on the scarf. However, it did not seem to work.

Second, Claudia sat next to Poppy again in French!

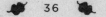

I wasn't sure how I was I supposed to react to this change in the seating plan. A one-off—such as accidentally tripping and falling into the seat next to Poppy—would have been forgivable, but unlikely to happen twice! Poppy did look apologetic as I walked in and beckoned for me to sit near her, but there weren't any seats. Instead I sat across the aisle next to Sasha, who nudged me halfway through the lesson.

"So, what do you think?" Sasha said cryptically.

I glanced cautiously at Miss Rustford, who was a bit fierce at the best of times, to see if she was looking in our direction.

"Of what?" I whispered.

"Of me snogging Darren last night!"

"Ssh!" Miss Rustford looked up from the front of the room, and then went back to obliterating some poor Year Seven's homework with red pen. Miss Rustford was a tough marker. There was a wild rumor she'd once given Susanna Forbes, the class overachiever, an A-minus, but no one really believed it.

I paused. "You didn't tell me that!" I whispered very quietly, under cover of extracting a pen from my bag.

"I texted you five minutes ago. You looked bored."

"I handed my phone in!"

Sasha just shook her head at me, which sent one of her plaited hair extensions right into my eye. Our Mobile Phone Debate was becoming a bit of a ritual. Sasha said I should keep my mobile on silent during lessons instead of obeying school rules and handing it in each day during morning registration. She said, how were you supposed to communicate with the person sitting next to you if not by exchanging text messages with your phone on silent? Sasha reveled in the covert reading and writing of mid-lesson texts, but I got scared of getting caught and having the message read out for everyone to hear. What if it was a fantasy one about snogging Luke?

Out of the corner of my noninjured eye I could see Claudia whispering something to Poppy. Poppy laughed.

"Claudia!" said Miss Rustford.

Claudia was impressively serene at being singled out. She just stared at Miss Rustford, whereas I would have retreated into red-faced embarrassment.

After school I went round to Poppy's to borrow her math textbook (forgot mine when my bag-packing coincided with a vivid Luke fantasy) and she was being weird. Weird! With me! She should have been extra nice to me after the Seating Incident!

"We can't go to the youth club on Friday," Poppy told me.

"What, your parents have made plans again?" I pushed a rogue sunflower seed back through the bars of Mouse's cage.

Poppy paused awkwardly. "No—I'm invited to a party in Lansdowne. It's Claudia's cousin Angela's seventeenth."

"Oh," I said, trying to convey complete indifference about not being invited. It was probably just as well I only needed one syllable.

"I wanted to ask if you could come too," said Poppy, "but, well, it's Claudia's cousin . . ."

"Right—"

"And I don't know her, so—"

"That's fine," I said. It came out in a small voice.

"I figured that you wouldn't be allowed to go, anyway," said Poppy.

Ouch. As if it was my fault that my mum was always keeping tabs on me! Poppy and I looked at each other in sudden silence. Poppy and I had always shared a desire for things to be more fun. But we'd been friends for years, ever since Ivy decided she was too cool to get the bus to school with me (apparently the only thing worse than a purple and gray school uniform being a little sister kitted out to match). Ivy had promptly abandoned me at the bus stop, where I met Poppy. Since then, we'd been inseparable. Unless the friendship had just been convenient all that time. . . .

"Is that a new hair clip?" I asked, to hide the knot of tension in my stomach. It was one I'd seen while window shopping. I could definitely buy it too, if it went into a miraculous 95-percent-off sale.

"It was a present from Claudia! She bought two and decided she didn't like one. Can you believe it?"

"That's great," I lied.

"She's so generous."

I was saved from commenting by Poppy's phone beeping. She texted something back, grinning. I looked intently at Mouse in order to demonstrate my complete lack of curiosity about who it was. I knew that one party with Claudia didn't spell the end of our friendship or anything, but usually if I was stuck at home reading my horoscope on a Friday night, at least Poppy was there too!

How to Win Friends and Influence People

IN ENGLISH ON WEDNESDAY WE DID THIS really cool poem by Browning called "Porphyria's Lover," where a bloke strangles a girl with her long hair. I was quite tempted to do the same to Claudia and then blame the bad influence of English literature when questioned on my motives by the police. When I thought about it objectively, Claudia was totally fake and annoying. It was amazing all that hair flicking didn't make her lose her balance—it was like watching a shampoo advert on fast forward half the time! What could Claudia contribute to a friendship? (Apart from, admittedly, invitations to cool social events, seduction tips, unwanted magazines with the free samples still inside, and annoyingly desirable hair clips.) It was so irritating that I could only half-heartedly join in the Year Nine skiing trip debates.

YEAR NINE SKIING TRIP CONCERNS

1. Whether the ski instructors would be good-looking.
2. Whether our hostel would also be hosting a Year Ten or Eleven boys' school group.
3. Whether it was true that in France you got served wine with every meal, even breakfast.

The real question was, what if Poppy and Claudia went off together during the skiing trip? It seemed increasingly likely. In geography, Poppy and Claudia sat next to each other again, removing any hope that the seating changes were limited to French lessons, and that Poppy's desertion was somehow linked to our differing aptitude at French oral. (I was crap but Claudia was really good—Latin roots and all that, which was clearly cheating.)

I took a deep breath and sat down just across the aisle from them, followed by Sasha, who silently assessed the situation, squeezed past my chair, and sat down next to me.

Miss Vine walked in the room, said, "Good afternoon, girls!" and started wiping off the extra large date that someone had written in green marker pen across the whiteboard. Everyone carried on talking. Claudia looked critically toward the front of the room and said in an undertone, "God, I think my mum's cleaner has got that skirt."

"Even Miss Rustford wouldn't wear that," said Poppy.

I thought of something sufficiently bitchy to join in with. "It looks like bus seat material!"

Poppy giggled and immediately leaned toward me. I felt better. Maybe Claudia just sat next to Poppy without asking and Poppy was actually really bored?

"Holly—do you remember that time in Year Eight?" Poppy finally managed to say between her giggles.

"What time?" I said casually, to emphasize to Claudia the many years of hilarious moments that Poppy and I had shared. And because I didn't know.

"That time when you"—Poppy was practically collapsing with laughter now—"called Miss Vine 'Mum' by mistake?"

Poppy and Claudia promptly dissolved into proper, can't-speak-I'm-so-funny type giggles, at which Miss

Vine said sharply, "Ssh!" But they just seemed delighted with their hilarity. Then I could see Claudia discreetly text something under her desk. A second later, Poppy jumped slightly and giggled. After Miss Vine had looked away again, Poppy slipped out her mobile from her blazer pocket, from where it had presumably been vibrating. I couldn't believe it. Poppy usually handed her phone in every morning, whereas Claudia always claimed to have forgotten hers so she could keep it. It looked as if Poppy was now being forgetful too! Poppy wasn't supposed to go off with someone else! We had joint New Year's resolutions, for God's sake!

Then Miss Vine announced at the end of the lesson that we were going to do mini-projects in pairs for the next fortnight's homework. D'oh! This made me Sasha's partner in a project called "Urban Car Usage." Which translated as, "Allow Poppy and Claudia to go off together even more, while Sasha disappears to see Darren and you stand in the street by yourself counting Ford Fiestas."

I wanted to ask Poppy and Claudia if I could join their group, but I knew that, annoyingly, it wouldn't make sense. Was it just me or did the world only operate in multiples of two? Four-player family games. Two decent bedrooms for Ivy and Jamie. Two people per project. I was used to it at home, but now I was beginning to feel the odd one out at school, too.

Sasha did, however, poke me in the side just as the bell went. "Holly, you see that globe on Miss Vine's desk?"

I looked up glumly. "Yes. So?"

"Do you want me to chuck it at Claudia's head?"

She can be really sweet sometimes.

ALTHOUGH THE WEEK HAD RAPIDLY GONE totally weird, neither Poppy nor I altered our bus-catching routine. It wasn't as if we'd actually flung any schoolbooks at each other or anything. Also, let's face it, the only other option was walking to school.

I was momentarily cheered up when I saw Luke on the bus on the way home on Thursday. He was downstairs at the back, an oasis of gorgeousness shrouded in a romantic, soft-focus haze! (Although that might have been someone's illicit cigarette smoke.) Poppy and I had to stand in the bus gangway because there weren't any seats, but I could still see Luke's dark curly hair through the throng of tiny Year Sevens with their huge school bags. I was tempted to fling aside my purple duffel coat, cast it carelessly into the luggage rack, and fight my way toward him in slow motion, but I held on to a handrail to stop myself.

When the bus was coming up to the stop near our road, Luke got up and we stood right next to each other by the doors! Then, we almost got off the bus at the same time except the door on my side stuck and took longer to open. If it weren't for that I could have said, "I got off with Luke," and it would have been true!

My dad is right that public transport is rubbish.

I COULD HAVE DONE WITH A LUKE-SIGHTING to cheer me up on Friday, but he didn't appear. I sat next to Charlotte in French (to prove I was not bothered by seating-related treachery) and slipped my mobile phone into my lap. It wasn't just Claudia who could nonchalantly break rules! I had carefully claimed to have forgotten my phone at handing-in time so that I could text Poppy. However, with a pang I remembered that it was the day of the stupid party, which meant

Poppy and Claudia would be planning their evening, with no need for anyone else's involvement.

Poppy turned and smiled at me from her seat next to Claudia, but I could only manage to smile back through gritted teeth. So I texted Sasha instead.

Have u started geog? I wrote painstakingly (no predictive text on my mobile, so everything took ages to spell out).

The reply came back ultra-quickly: "**What was geog again?**"

I typed, "**Never mind**" and hit Send.

"**U txting in lessons now?**"

I drew a smiley face: "**:-)**"

Sasha replied: "**Is that the stupid hair clip?**"

I felt the warm, reassuring glow of shared dislike. I looked at Miss Rustford, busy scribbling illegibly on the whiteboard, then wrote: "**U would either have 2 b mad or b bribed 2 b friends with C, ha ha!**" I added another smiley face, then wondered for a little while which symbols would illustrate a face puking in disgust. Unfortunately, before I could decide, a shadow fell across my desk, and on life as I knew it.

"*Mademoiselle* Stockwell?"

Oh God. I looked up. Miss Rustford was standing

over me! That sarcastic "*mademoiselle*" thing was always a bad sign.

"I'll have that mobile phone please," she said icily.

I looked around the room and thought, God, I hate being in trouble. Everyone looks at you. That's mainly why I revise for tests, do homework, etc. Being quietly diligent really helps avoid unwelcome attention. My only glimmer of hope was that Miss Rustford would somehow find the mercy to ignore school rules and let me off with a warning for a first time offense, rather than go the whole hog and read out the message! Unfortunately, my glimmer of hope had obviously run off with my guardian angel for a day out at the seaside. Everyone looked up with sudden interest as Miss Rustford began reading, very slowly and deliberately. "You would either have to be mad or be bribed to be friends with C—"

I felt sick as Poppy and Claudia spun round, in synchronized outrage.

Miss Rustford stopped and looked stonily at me, without even reading the "ha ha."

"Mademoiselle Stockwell, you can consider this phone confiscated!"

What happened to fourteen being a good age?

 48

One Hundred Years of Solitude

I REALIZE THERE WAS A FATAL FLAW IN MY IDEA about abolishing Mondays. Tuesday would feel like the new Monday. In fact, all available days would have to be turned into holidays in order to abolish the dread of a school day ahead. I am sure the Prime Minister will have been through this exact same train of thought at some point, except not in so much detail since he has never had to put up with Poppy, Claudia, and Miss Rustford. Sasha was no help when I spent the weekend in the hall, head in my hands, whispering repeatedly into the phone, "Oh God, why did I write that text?"

"Well, don't worry, at least you let them know how you felt," said Sasha, who was a big believer in Saying Things to People's Faces.

"But I didn't want them to know how I felt!" I said. "I just want things to be back to normal." I hate that feeling of open warfare, it makes me feel uneasy and sick. I just wanted my nice, safe life back.

That Monday, Poppy and I still managed the exact same daily bus journeys together, just accompanied by our two new friends, Tension and Treachery. I wanted to rant at her about her behavior, but I didn't want to make things worse and really mess everything up, so I actually just read my book, even though reading on the bus makes me feel sick. Meanwhile Poppy didn't say much either, unless it was to make a subtle dig. Or perhaps comment about how cool it was that Claudia had so many interesting stories and could go out whenever she wanted. I refused to ask Poppy how the party had been on Friday night. I could imagine it, anyway. Probably a big, decadent event full of gorgeous boys where Poppy and Claudia giggled a lot and bonded over both getting drunk or pregnant or something else that simply wouldn't befall you if you spent Friday night in your room looking under your bed for lost socks. I couldn't even text Sasha to prove I had other friends, since my phone had been confiscated by Miss Rustford for a whole week! I am sure that infringes on my human rights. That is not even in the school rules, which proves how monstrous and power-crazed she is.

After we got off the bus, Poppy turned to look at me accusingly. "Did you tell people you and Luke watched a sunset from the top of a snow-covered hill?"

"Of course not!" Honestly, you can't say anything in our year without it being blown out of all proportion. And what did Luke have to do with anything?

"Claudia heard you tell Rashida those exact words," said Poppy, scrutinizing me as we entered the newsagent's for our daily chocolate dose. "After everyone was looking at my photos."

"It was just a joke to Sasha," I said, with only a slight trace of defensiveness. "Luke and I did spend time together when it snowed."

"Holly, you slid down Kestrel Hill together *once* on bin liners."

"And that must have *bin* meaningful for him?"

Poppy gave me a withering glance.

I sighed and attempted an honest, cards-on-the-table moment. "Does he hate me then?"

Big mistake.

"No," said Poppy as her phone played out a loud

polyphonic medley. "He just thinks you're weird. Hi, Clauds!"

Weird? Even the newsagent winced when she said it.

I knew Poppy was just annoyed about the text, but still. I wasn't sure I liked her at all anymore—I got the feeling she was just being purposefully horrible, as if it was fun to ruin my life. One minute everything had been fine and the next it had all been pulled out from under my feet. I felt like saying something, but kept my mouth shut. Poppy was already going off all the time with Claudia. It would hardly encourage her to spend more time with me if I started being confrontational. At least this way I could just ignore it and then when it blew over it would be as if it never happened.

Just when I thought things couldn't possibly get any worse, I fell off the curb while crossing the road and two small children laughed at me.

TEN DAYS LATER, LIFE TRULY TOOK ON THE same security as a bathroom with no lock. I thought it was bad enough that Poppy and Claudia had been constantly texting, speaking in baby voices, and disappearing together on secret missions! (I kept having to pretend to be immersed in drawing flowcharts, writing down vocab, etc., which was quite accomplished acting.)

But then it got worse. One Wednesday morning, Poppy and Claudia sat behind me in computing, chatting loudly and saying, "Shall we tell her the bad news now or later?" I was selectively deaf, like Mum when Jamie asks if she has any potato chips, and carried on with my typing exercise. Our computing teacher, Miss Stevenson, insisted on giving us typing tests, as if it was the 1950s and we were all going to be secretaries when we grew up. Sasha hated it because she was really bad at it and always got bad marks, but I actually didn't mind it. There was something satisfying about being able to type fast without even needing to look at the screen. It was really convenient. The faster you finished the exercise, the more free time you had to covertly check your e-mails on the Internet and sulk about Poppy and Claudia. Those two were really making me wish I was a superhero. Not like Jamie jumping down the stairs thinking he could fly (although actually I agree flying would be cool), more in the sense of having a secret identity as an invisible crime fighter. At least then I could wander around being the one with no friends but in a cool "I'm in a film and the underdog will prevail" type way. Rather than actually just wandering around with no friends.

Anyway, the bad news was revealed just before French. When Poppy and Claudia sat down across the aisle, Claudia pulled my sleeve to get my attention.

"Hello!" she said.

"Hello," I replied, cautiously.

Claudia nudged Poppy, who contributed, "How's it going?"

"Fine," I said back. (Subtext: apart from you turning into a monster.)

Claudia sighed, looked at Poppy, then announced, "Did you know I'm staying over at Poppy's on Friday?"

I clearly didn't, so that was hardly a proper question. And I wasn't invited? What an insult. I flashed a look at Poppy, then looked away again when she made eye contact, struggling to suppress my feelings. How could she do this to me? I mean, I know I'd written that stupid text. But surely she understood that I was just hurt! I knew our friendship didn't lead to exciting invitations, friends in Year Ten, free stuff, etc., but I thought I could rely on her!

Then, Claudia chose to break the real news.

"It'll be great to meet Luke. We'll probably all get pizza and watch a DVD."

My stomach lurched. Please God, no. *Claudia* was going to get together with *Luke*? Claudia is so stunning and tall and sultry—basically my opposite. At best, I can pass for normal. If my mouth is closed so you can't see my braces.

"Great!" I lied, fantasizing fondly about shoving my ruler up her nose.

"Do you think Luke will let me see his DVD collection?" Claudia continued loudly to Poppy. I saw with horror that Claudia was writing *C loves L* in pen on her desk. "I always wanted to be a film director when I was little."

I wanted to look at Poppy again but knew I would give myself away by looking really hurt. How could she allow this to happen? I know I tried to stop her making embarrassing comments about me and Luke, but she knew how much I liked him! Instead I occupied myself by laughing loudly at something Sasha had said. Which only alarmed Sasha, as she'd been asking Charlotte if there was an accent in "*recevoir.*"

I T WAS INCALCULABLY CRUEL THAT ON Thursday evening, in my traumatized state, I was dragged to watch Mum, Dad, and Jamie play badminton, when surely there was no better timing for a rendezvous with my duvet. As Mum put on her latest pair of new white trainers, I thought, Should I just tell her I don't want to go? No, surely she already knew deep down that I didn't want to, but persisted in urging me to go along as if she could inject athleticism into me. I didn't want to upset her by hammering home the point that one of her children wasn't as talented or keen as the rest of them, and that we didn't have anything in common, when it was so obviously important to her. So I went along and sat at the side.

I went to get my phone out from pure habit, then remembered a) it was confiscated and b) I wasn't speaking to Poppy. With the support structure of my friends gone, watching badminton was—well, watching badminton. How depressing! I got out my rough book:

THINGS I AM NOW SERIOUSLY WORRIED ABOUT

1. What if Poppy and I still aren't speaking and she goes off with Claudia on the skiing trip next week?

I can't imagine seducing gorgeous teenage ski instructors without Poppy acting like she is an expert because of Yves.

2. What if Claudia tells Luke that her mum is an actress and he thinks that is really cool and snogs her passionately?

3. What if I end up all by myself and have to help Miss Rustford hand out worksheets?

4. Who am I going to sit next to on the coach?

F OR A BRIEF MOMENT AFTER I GOT BACK from badminton I thought everything would be okay because Poppy unexpectedly came round! However, she just wanted to pick up Luke's scarf. Drat. At the door Poppy sort of opened and closed her mouth and shuffled around a bit so I thought that she might fling herself at my feet sobbing and saying that she was sorry, and that of course she wouldn't let Claudia go near Luke, but she didn't actually say anything. So I primly suggested she stay outside while I got the scarf, in order to be Officially Distant. And so she didn't see me retrieve it from under my pillow.

I ended up trying to watch *EastEnders* while

Mum did her yoga in front of the TV. Unfortunately *EastEnders* had a "young romance" storyline that was both a) mortifying and b) deeply depressing, especially when one of the characters bought a Valentine's card.

Oh God.

Valentine's Day was in a few days' time!

I stared at the TV and thought, Please let me get a card! But I didn't know any available boys, apart from Luke and Evil Liam. And Claudia's ambitions meant Luke would no doubt be buying her one. Unless someone on the bus had secretly fallen in love with me, found out where I lived, and thought, "I know, I'll buy her a card."

"That girl should watch out," announced Mum to the TV, never having clearly defined the boundaries between reality and fiction. "That boy will probably get her pregnant and then find somebody else."

God, how cringeworthy. She might as well have added, "Just as well we sent you to an all-girls school, eh, Holly?" I've never been able to talk to Mum about my life. Can you imagine it? I would get the following snippets from *Mum's Book of Really Crap Advice:*

1. I am too young to be worrying about all that.
2. Friends who play stupid games aren't proper friends at all.
3. I should rise above it.
4. (Irrelevant, but added for good measure): Have I considered getting some fresh air?

FRIDAY NIGHT.

Claudia was busy stealing the only boy I had ever loved.

I had a rendezvous with my math homework.

I drew a flowchart in my rough book of the likelihood of ever sitting next to Luke in the back of his parents' car again. It didn't look good. Then I tried to watch TV to avoid thinking at all. Unfortunately I kept getting mental images of Luke snogging Claudia and saying, "Oooh, I love your untangly hair," or, "A film director? Me too!" Eventually I decided I might as well do that geography project. Sasha was never going to do it and I urgently needed to numb my brain as completely as possible.

I told Mum I was going out. She evidently decided that people didn't usually sneak off to meet boys holding a pen and a geography textbook, because she just said, "Okay then. Take your phone for security." I didn't dare tell her that it had run out of credit again thanks to a long chat with Sasha on the way home to celebrate its return from confiscation. Oh well. It was chunky enough to physically knock out the average mugger anyway.

I walked down my street and turned onto Rosehill Road. One blue car, three red, one yellow. Done!

I was almost home again before I looked at my notes and realized Miss Vine had been going on about different *types* of cars, not colors. (Why? How was this useful?) So I walked back again, peering at the logos on the cars. One blue Ford Focus. Three red Nissan Micras . . . aargh!

Poppy, Claudia, and Luke were walking down the other side of the road!

I ducked ultraquickly behind a parked Nissan Micra, before they saw me on my own on a Friday night. No, worse—on my own, *counting cars*.

Luke was wearing a big winter coat with a lovely fake-fur-lined hood that made him look like an Arctic explorer. He was walking quite fast in front of them. Maybe they were all going to a party? It looked as if

Poppy had straightened out her curls to match Claudia's permanently sleek hair, but she didn't look hugely dressed up. However Claudia was striding along in boots and a tiny black dress under a denim jacket. Oh God—what if they were going to the cinema or ice skating or something? That would give Claudia definite sitting-next-to- or clinging-on-to-Luke opportunities. She was a great skater but she would definitely pretend to be crap.

Suddenly Claudia bounded up to Luke, leaving Poppy walking behind! I edged round the car in order to see better, then wished I hadn't. Claudia's arm was threaded into Luke's! She was lucky he wasn't jumping onto a balcony, holding roses, driving her around on a motorbike, or anything else on my Favorite Fantasies list, or I would have had to run across and whack her with my geography book.

"I love your coat!" I heard Claudia tell Luke.

Despair crashed over me. I felt like running in slow motion toward them, screaming "Nooooo! I like the coat more!"

I couldn't see Luke's face because he had his hood up, but he was doubtless smiling and thinking how lovely/exotic/glamorous (tick all that apply) she was.

They had reached the corner now, by the newsagent's. There were no more parked cars on my side of the road so I couldn't get any closer.

They all had some sort of discussion, then Poppy went into the newsagent's by herself. Oh God. Poppy had left Claudia and Luke alone! On a dark street! Was she mad? I hated not knowing what was going on. Claudia was saying something and looking around. But most annoyingly, she still had her arm through Luke's!

I had a choice: kneel behind the car watching Claudia seduce the man of my dreams, or go home for an urgent appointment with a chocolate bar. I paused for a moment, hoping to see Luke run away at high speed, but he didn't. I wandered home in an unhappy daze, thinking about how awful everyone would feel if I died in an accident or something. They'd be sorry at my funeral that they weren't nicer to me, wouldn't they?

Extra-depressingly, Monday meant both Valentine's Day and swimming. My swimming cap was really sprouting leaks these days. The thing is, you could patch over the holes, but it would never be the same. Like my love life.

The Water Babies

AFTER A PRETTY BLACK WEEKEND, I WAS somehow still in one piece. Although, by the time Sasha turned up to English on Monday, the only spare desk was on the other side of the room, scandalously depriving us of a Valentine's Day bulletin.

"No cards," I managed to mouth, halfway through the lesson.

Sasha pulled a face and mouthed, "Text from Darren—crap."

Susanna Forbes was reading in full drama school mode, putting loads of expression into the dialogue as if she was going to be rapidly accelerated through school, into Oxford, and out the other end with a first class degree at the age of fourteen.

"That's my last Duchess painted on the wall . . ."

I saw Poppy surreptitiously roll her eyes at Bethan, who she was, oddly, sitting next to instead of Claudia. I thought, I wonder if Poppy got a card from Jez? Not that I cared.

I caught Sasha's eye and mouthed, "Darren's just being rubbish."

I knew just enough about boys (well, from books) to be aware that even if you managed to snog one several times, they were still very bad at sending cards and being romantic. Mind you, I bet Claudia had received loads of cards. I looked over. She looked as self-satisfied as ever, as if permanently pleased by how alluring she was. I pulled a face at my rough book and revised one of my lists:

THINGS BOYS ARE USELESS AT

1. Sending Valentine's cards.
2. Spending money on good things instead of buying models of cars, little pots of metallic paint, etc.
3. Realizing the love of their life is RIGHT THERE, living on the same street as them.
4. Eating quietly.

"Sasha?" said Mrs. Mitford finally, after allowing Susanna to continue reading for far longer than everyone else.

Sasha adopted a pained grimace and resignedly began to read.

I N SWIMMING, I KEPT FIGHTING THE URGE to just sit underwater in despair at the whole situation (no cards, no Luke, no friends to sit with on imminent skiing trip). Mind you, I could hardly have drowned myself in three centimeters of water. There has always been a strict swimming hierarchy at our school:

The **A** Group	Allowed to dive off the diving board. Can do butterfly stroke and then look all nonchalant, as if it is no effort whatsoever.
The **B** Group	Good enough to go in the deep end. Can do breaststroke or front crawl.
The **C (Crap)** Group	Only permitted in shallow end. Are surrounded by as many polystyrene floats as possible. Might manage a halfhearted doggy paddle.

Only myself and Jo McAllister had managed to maintain our position in the Crap Swimming Group since Year Seven. A's and B's were always at the scary, freezing-cold deep end, ready to dive in, while Jo and I would just walk up and down the shallow end, knees bent, with a white polystyrene float under each arm. (Once they tried to merge us with the B Group, but we used armbands on our ankles and got successfully relegated before the lesson was over.) Jo is totally lovely, but for some reason she is friends with Claudia. Must be because Jo's parents drive her and Claudia to school each day from Lansdowne.

Halfway through the lesson, Mrs. Mastiff's attention was diverted by Rashida (a B) nearly having had her eye taken out by Claudia (an A) doing butterfly without having removed her silver charm bracelet from Mike (an X). Jo and I leaned against the side of the pool and hoped Mrs. Mastiff wouldn't notice we had stopped. Mrs. Mastiff reserved a special kind of hatred for me, because Ivy had been her star pupil. She took my lack of ability as a personal insult—though at least she never mixed us up.

I adjusted my leaky swimming cap. "I need a new one of these," I said to Jo. It kept making my hair go all tangly. Jo never had any trouble with hers. Anyway, she has curly auburn hair that doesn't tangle or look silly even if it does get wet.

"You can't see the patches that much," said Jo kindly, in her soft Scottish accent.

Maybe it did actually look okay? I wondered. Jo was usually reliably blunt.

"I didn't get any Valentine's cards—did you?" I asked, picking at my polystyrene float. It hurt that I wasn't having this conversation with Poppy. We'd gone from sharing everything to sharing nothing.

"Nope." Jo paused to flick away a used Band-Aid that was bobbing near her chin. "Mind you, Claudia only got one."

"One?" I tried to keep the surprise from my voice. I continued, casually, "You would have thought she'd get loads." Obviously, I was careful when talking to Jo about Claudia, but I wanted to find out, so I added, "You know, from the blokes at her fencing club, and at that party the other week, and . . ."

Jo looked puzzled. "What, her cousin Angela's party? No—I was there. It wasn't that thrilling. Her aunt and uncle were there the whole time! Claudia kept telling Angela how crap it was."

That was interesting! But I needed to hear more Valentine's news. "So—the card?"

"Oh—yes. It was from this eleven-year-old who lives next door to her!"

But . . . what about Luke? What on earth was going on?

MAJOR SHOCK! CLAUDIA AND LUKE WERE not an item after all! Somehow, it had gone wrong! Well, not totally, ultrasatisfyingly wrong—Luke didn't push Claudia in a big pile of manure or anything—but none of her lipstick had besmirched his lips! No snog outside the newsagent's after all . . . ! Bethan told me this after history. I knew something subtle had changed when Claudia sat down next to Bethan in the lesson. Then, when Poppy came in and glanced toward the back where they were, Claudia and Bethan appeared to be deep in conversation! Poppy saw me following her gaze and sheepishly sat next to me! We couldn't talk or pass notes because we were right at the front, but it felt like normality might be returning.

I was torn for a minute while I considered what to do. Should I simply be glad of the apparent ceasefire, or should I turn away so Poppy would know how it felt? I had a little think. But finally, I decided that it would only lead to more unpleasantness. Getting a normal world back was what I had wanted all along, wasn't it? And it was the skiing trip tomorrow. It would be much better to swallow my pride than prolong the argument and risk being on bad terms while we were away. So I did nothing, and thought about what clothes to pack instead.

Innocents Abroad

A
FTER ALL THAT, I HAD TO SQUEEZE
months of skiing anticipation into one night. I
was still hoping to avoid the actual skiing, but
I could still get excited. After all, it was my first time
abroad, unless the Isle of Wight counted! My anticipation
was interrupted somewhat by Mum, who kept distracting
me from packing by coming into my room with empty
travel-size bottles. Do I look like I would want to spend
£4.99 on Body Shop conditioner in order to decant it
into an old drugstore hand cream tub? She left a neatly
arranged pile on the end of my bed consisting of:

Tube of antiseptic cream

Three safety pins pinned onto a bandage

Miniature sewing kit containing: one miniature

needle threader, two needles, and lengths of
black, white, and gray cotton
Deep Heat after-exercise spray

All I really needed was an extra tub of lip balm to
aid post-snogging lip maintenance after encounters
with the seductive Year Ten boys that were bound to be
sharing our hostel. Not that I would have told her that.

I GOT ON THE COACH OUTSIDE SCHOOL AFTER
an innocent hug good-bye from Mum, which
turned out to be her slipping a travel pack of Wet
Wipes and a sports bandage into the back pocket of my
rucksack. I had my mind on more troubling matters,
though; where you sit on a coach is always such a
political nightmare:

Avoid at all costs	Why?
Front of the coach	The teachers sit there (and Susanna Forbes)
Back of the coach	Reserved by scary, cool people

I sat down in safe mid-coach territory, just in front of Charlotte and Bethan. Poppy was one of the last onboard, clutching anti-travel-sickness tablets and a birthday present from her parents, to be opened on our last day. Claudia was at the back, chatting animatedly to Cool Tanya. Poppy sat next to me again!

Now it was definitely possible to talk properly. I wasn't going to start, though.

Surprisingly, Poppy immediately started chatting about Jez, as if we were Suddenly Back to Normal! She told me in detail about how she did intend to send Jez a Valentine's card. Apparently she read an article in *CosmoGIRL!* about how to do it subtly and was going to get her cousin in Exeter to post it so Jez wouldn't be able to guess by the postmark who it was from, but then chickened out from sending it. Which might have been a bit *too* subtle. Poppy was going to text while we were skiing, instead, and we needed to start planning what she was going to write.

It was all a bit weird at first. I was really having trouble with being back to normal when things had been so odd between us! There were loads of questions I wanted to ask. How could you go off with Claudia like that? What happened with Claudia and Luke? Are you only sitting next to me because Claudia didn't look up when you got on the coach? I wanted to tell Poppy that she'd hurt me; that she and Claudia had got me into such a downward spiral that I had accidentally missed a repeat of *Friends*, which wouldn't do, even if it was just one of those episodes made up of flashbacks. But there were other things I wanted to know too. How was it going with Jez? What DVDs had Luke recently bought? What tops had Poppy packed? And, to be honest, it was just really nice to have her back. So I kept quiet.

"What would you rather . . . ," Poppy began suddenly, "suck cold chicken soup through an old sock you found in the street or drink five pints of moldy milk?"

"I wouldn't do either," I said. I was playing a game on my phone—my favorite. It is called Worm and is basically the easiest game in the world. You just guide a little worm around the screen eating bonus coins and avoiding walls.

"If you HAD to. No choice."

"Erm . . . moldy milk."

"Ugh!" Poppy wrinkled her nose.

"Score!" I shouted. My worm had done well. The phone managed a rudimentary beep of congratulations as I continued. "What would you rather . . . lick the floor of the bus where someone has vomited—or sit next to people with really smelly armpits for the rest of your life?"

"Hmm—smelly armpits."

"Yuck!" No, it definitely wasn't worth asking any of the really unpleasant questions about Claudia. What was the point of chatting happily about vomit, then messing it up with an uncomfortable discussion? We didn't get round to any text planning, either—Poppy decided to see if there were any good flirting tips in *CosmoGIRL!* magazine.

After going through the Eurotunnel we spent hours and hours driving to the Alps. Poppy looked back at Claudia a few times, then got bored and began shouting, "*Bonjour* nice om!" and waving at cars whenever she saw a good-looking bloke in a car. When Miss Rustford wearily requested that she stop practicing her French on alarmed motorists, Poppy sat back down and started taking Charlotte and Bethan through the photos on her phone. She skimmed through several close-ups of her own toes that I had already seen—"I was worried that they looked wonky," Poppy reiterated—and then suddenly Charlotte went, "Oh, is that one of Luke and Claudia?"

I focused in very quickly on Poppy's phone, my stomach lurching at the thought that I had rejoiced prematurely and was about to see a "God-you're-stunning, marry-me-now" type embrace on the little screen. (I was just allowing thoughts of Luke back into my head—far too difficult to manage while I thought he was getting together with Claudia.)

Interestingly, the photo was mainly of Luke. He was leaning his head away from a grinning Claudia, looking a bit uncomfortable! It appeared she was trying her best to lean close to him! Charlotte raised her eyebrows at me and smiled. I maturely kept any delight from showing in my face.

MY SKI BADGE SAID *ECOLE DE SKI DES Montagnes Blanches: Groupe débutant*, which was French for Crap Group. On the first day skiing, Miss Rustford took Claudia and the others with their own skis to do dramatic red runs or something like that up on the mountain. Everyone else had to get all goggled up *au* Michelin Man by Mrs. Mastiff and the rental shop assistants. Instead of employing a fit instructor for the beginners, Mrs. Mastiff had decided to do the classes herself! It turned out she'd done some stupid course last summer. You'd think a grown woman would have had something better to do with a summer holiday, considering she must be allowed out in London, on holiday with her friends, etc. We were all absolutely gutted. Even more so when we found out there weren't any fit boys in our hostel either, just middle-aged Germans! So, no boy action at all, except when a middle-aged bloke wolf-whistled at Claudia. In fact, I only knew that because Bethan told me. When we arrived, Claudia pestered Miss Rustford to let her share a hostel room with the Year Tens, since one of Cool Tanya's friends had dropped out at the last minute, which meant Poppy, Charlotte, Bethan, Rashida, and I were all together and would hardly see anything of Claudia. (Hurrah!)

Poppy wrote a postcard to Jez. She was going to text him, but there was no reception on anyone's phone up in the mountains. It was not surprising, really, since the whole place felt like the eighteenth century. In our bit of the resort there were no cinemas or clothes shops or actual fun things to do—the only option was skiing! Also, the hostel rooms were really basic, with four rickety bunk beds per room and one big sofa bed that we all fought over (and Poppy got it because it was her birthday on the last day). So much for warming my toes on a furry rug in front of a roaring log fire! That must only be in James Bond films.

The card took about three hours to write because Poppy kept sitting around going, "Should I send him one or not?" with the blank card in front of her. It was funny—she could chat away to Jez at a hundred miles an hour, but when it came to writing she was a mess. Whereas for me, it was the talking I couldn't do, over-whelmed with the sense of how crucial it was that they liked me and that I sounded cool.

"He definitely fancies you," I said. "Of course you should." I hoped Poppy was appreciative of how helpful I was being, despite the Claudia Betrayal. That still hurt. But every time I thought about it, two voices in my head had a little argument. Would it really be a good idea to drag the whole subject into the daylight? No way. It would risk a big argument that might leave me back with no friends at all. My feelings about it were too messy. So I left them buried, where they couldn't do any damage.

"Jez is always making fun of me, though," said Poppy, biting her pink-inked gel pen.

"Yes, but he's a *boy*," I said. "It's . . . you know, like Gilbert."

"What?"

"In *Anne of Green Gables*. This character Gilbert pulls Anne's hair and calls her names. It's his way of expressing that he likes her."

"And do they get together?"

"Yes."

"Really?"

"Well, not straight away. But in the end."

Poppy looked unconvinced, so I changed tack.

"Did you find tips in any magazines?"

Poppy's expression brightened. "Yes." She rummaged and produced a crumpled page. "'Long Distance Lurve.' From *CosmoGIRL!*. Last September's issue."

Poppy's magazine archive was staggering. I'd seen the pile next to her bed.

"Messages to make him melt . . . ," I read out loud. "Make sure your saucy reunion sizzles like a sausage on a beach barbecue!"

Poppy looked a bit scared. I sifted through her postcards, still blank except for the addresses. "Have you got spares?"

She nodded.

"Well, for *example*, I could write this to the *luurrvely* Luke."

I wrote on his card in big pink swirly letters: *Luke,* mon amour. *How are you,* mon cheri? *We are having a lush time here in the Alps. Wish you were here (in my bedroom—oh la la!) Love and French kisses, Holly.*

Giggling, Poppy tried to grab the pen from me as I elaborated with lots of big kisses, which trailed wonkily up the side of the card.

"Okay! I get the picture. Vividly." Poppy carefully wrote on Jez's card, "Hi, Jez. Holly and I are having a great time skiing. The food is nice. See you soon, Poppy."

"Why not 'love, Poppy'?"

"No!"

I put Luke's card down, thinking of what I really wanted to say, just like in all those unsent text messages: *Luke, you are divine. Thank you for not going out with Claudia. Please decide I'm not weird and ask me out. Love, Holly.*

BEFORE TOO LONG, I COULD THINK OF nothing but how much I ached. We kept getting up really early each morning for a breakfast of fresh baguettes and bowls of hot chocolate in the nice warm hostel (fab), then walking up a mountain in order to fall over repeatedly in the snow (not fab).

One evening we were allowed out en masse for a walk and our coach driver Peter came along too. Without his coach! We went to a café for Coca-Colas and Miss Rustford had wine! By her third glass even she seemed to soften around the edges.

We all kept an eye out for fit boys but there weren't any. None! And I don't understand where this perception comes from that French people dress stylishly. Everyone I saw was wearing a fluorescent rucksack with the straps over both arms like they were part of a group of overgrown toddlers. Then we went to a shop and made Poppy stand outside so we could buy her some chocolate instead of a birthday cake for the last night. We discovered that Twixes and KitKats were about three times the price they are in England! Maybe that is the real reason French people don't get that fat. I bet it is the same in Italy and scientists have got the wrong end of the stick going on about olive oil.

DIDN'T DO TOO WELL AT AVOIDING SKIING. I kept getting swept up in the routine of getting all dressed up, negotiating the scary rope lift, etc., and then before I knew it I would be at the top of a slope, expected to ski down! The worst was on Saturday—our last day—when Mrs. Mastiff made us all do races in pairs! Five points for winning, two points for making it down the hill without falling over. (As if.)

"I'm going to mess it up," I said to Poppy in the queue, feeling panic-stricken. "How can my family actually enjoy this sort of thing?"

"You'll be fine. Just make sure you don't fall onto your ski poles, because you could get impaled and—"

"Oh God. We're too near the front. I should queue at the back."

"But who will I go with?" said Poppy, looking around in concern. Everyone was in pairs.

"Don't worry, I'll stay here then," I said. Another two people went and we all shuffled along in the queue toward our fate. I saw Poppy glance toward Claudia and I couldn't help saying, "I wouldn't leave you here all by yourself!"

Poppy sheepishly drew a shape in the snow with her ski pole and I felt like adding, "What kind of friend would that make me?" In fact, there was a lot more I could have said, most of which I'd already voiced in imaginary conversations. Poppy wasn't queuing with Claudia, but was that just because

Claudia was blanking her now that things didn't appear to be happening with Luke? How did I know Poppy wouldn't just do it again the next week? I wondered if I should just have it out with her properly, instead of dropping hints and never finding out for sure. The sense of unfairness was welling up inside me, big time. I opened my mouth and said, "Poppy—"

"What?" she said, catching the serious tone of my voice.

But I couldn't do it. First, it was her birthday, and second, I didn't really want to confront it all and start an argument, especially just before hurtling down a mountain. Perhaps I was being too sensitive, or childish. No one wanted a friend like that, did they?

"I've got an idea!" I said instead.

"What?"

I lay down in the snow. "Cover me with snow so Mrs. Mastiff doesn't see me!"

I was quite inspired. I was far less likely to mess up the skiing if I could avoid taking part!

"No, no—cover me too!" said Poppy, lying down as well.

"What are you doing?" said Charlotte, turning round to peer at us. Poppy explained and got Charlotte and Bethan to cover us both with snow. I think it was Poppy who got the giggles first, because she set me off and we lay there practically crying with laughter. The laughing suddenly felt stupidly good, as if all the suspicion and tension of the past few weeks was fading right to the back of my head.

Unfortunately our becoming invisible tactic didn't work, because Mrs. Mastiff shouted, "You two! Get up and get over here!"

I stood reluctantly at the start line and felt really, overwhelmingly faint. It was a beautiful, crisp day. The sky was a really gorgeous, intense blue, as if someone had colored it in with a blue felt tip pen (and not, for a change, as if the felt tip pen had run out halfway through). I really didn't want to kill myself by accident. There is a reason why I prefer relaxing pursuits to active ones. There are a vast number of sports-related injuries each year, whereas when was the last time you heard of a Twix-related injury?

"Go!" yelled Mrs. Mastiff.

Poppy went, but my legs had stopped working. Mrs. Mastiff walked up and I thought she would be all shouty, but instead she pushed me!

Oh my God.

I accelerated really fast. It all happened so quickly that something miraculous happened—I stayed up! If only someone had taken a photo—my mum would have been delighted. Before I knew it, the barrier was coming up. I quickly summoned up everything that I had learned and fell over in order to stop.

I lay there in a daze, looking at the nice blue sky while Mrs. Mastiff skied down the slope especially to lean over me.

"Get up, Holly."

"I feel faint," I told her.

"Your heart rate is up, that's all," Mrs. Mastiff said acidly. "It means you're actually exercising."

"You pushed me!" I said. Mrs. Mastiff just sighed and skied away.

I am sure I could sue her for that, you know.

O N THE LAST NIGHT WE ALL STAYED UP late after dinner so Poppy could open her birthday presents. She seemed to really like the Body Shop shower gel I'd bought in her favorite fragrance. Charlotte, Bethan, and Rashida had clubbed together to get a box of posh chocolates, while Poppy's mum and dad gave her a new pair of jeans and some money in an envelope! Just money, no strings attached. No accompanying pictures of hiking boots or exercise bikes or anything! I wish I had her parents.

Then our room stayed up even later to play Truth or Dare, which turned into a big True Confessions session where everyone talked about snogging and how far they had gone. Poppy told everyone else that she did really, *really* like Jez.

"We have never done anything, though," she said. "It's like, we're just good mates. He put his arm around me once, but that's it."

"He didn't, like, slip his hand down your top at the same time?" chipped in Charlotte. We all stared at her.

"Toby?" I asked. (Charlotte's ex.)

Charlotte nodded and giggled. "In the cinema. I did this sort of surprised squeak and had to pretend I had been scared by the film." She stopped to snort with laughter.

"Sshh!" hissed Bethan, who was on teacher-watch by the door.

"He said he thought I had popcorn on me and he was trying to brush it off!" Charlotte whispered.

Huh. When it was my turn there was a thunderous

silence because I didn't have any stories to tell. Poppy eventually interrupted this by saying, "Claudia tells this hilarious story about her first snog!" and then she launched into a tale which revolved around an entire fencing team fancying Claudia during some tournament, which helped her win, after which the opposing team's gorgeous, young instructor told her she looked like a cross between Cleopatra and a Bond girl, then snogged her.

Hmm. Poppy and I were the only ones that hadn't had boyfriends. It was okay while there were two of us, like when you're weren't the only one who failed a math test. But what if Poppy got together with Jez? It was bound to happen sooner or later. Then I would be the only inexperienced one left! (Even Miss Rustford's love life seemed to be getting somewhere. I was sure she had been wearing eyeshadow the other evening. And I heard Peter call her "Susan"!)

Suddenly, all this was put firmly into perspective.

"Has anyone seen a couple of postcards?" I heard Poppy ask in a low voice. "They had pink writing. They're gone. I thought they were next to my bed."

"Oh, don't worry," said Rashida. "I posted them for you."

Great Expectations

SOME SENTENCES ARE ALWAYS REALLY, really bad. For example, "Didn't you realize when you wore those white trousers that your period was due?" Well, "I posted them for you" was worse. Rashida saw my joke postcard to Luke on the floor and kindly posted it along with Poppy's one to Jez! Apparently Poppy owed her some money for the stamps. Jesus. So my card was on its way to England, Luke was going to know I was a loopy nutter who wanted to French kiss him, and I would be forced to combust from embarrassment.

All in all, I was a bit stressed! On the way home we got stuck in traffic while the coach became slowly fragranced with the Camembert cheese everyone had bought as a souvenir. Claudia spent the whole journey talking loudly at the back of the coach about the advantages of traveling by plane. Even the annoying sound of her voice couldn't keep me from panicking about the postcard problem. Could I phone Royal Mail Customer Services and ask them politely if they could lose it? When we had a quick break at a service station, I called Sasha on my mobile to ask her about it.

"You're back!" she said immediately. "God—was it a nightmare?"

"Well—Mrs. Mastiff pushed me down a mountain, and—"

"No, not the skiing! I already reckoned that would have been traumatic. I mean, with Poppy and Claudia and the whole not-speaking thing? I'm so sorry I'm not there to glare at them for you."

Oh.

"No," I said feebly, moving away from the rest of the group. "Poppy and I are friends now, it's fine. Claudia's gone off with the Year Tens again."

"So, did Poppy apologize?" asked Sasha.

"Well, no—but they've stopped going off together now and things with Poppy are back to how they were before—that's what I wanted, really."

Sasha paused, and then said, "Well, okay then."

I could tell she didn't get it. But Sasha and I were really different, sometimes. Having friends was really important, wasn't it? Even if sometimes they did stuff that upset you?

Anyway, I couldn't think about it right now, with the Postcard on the loose.

I tried hard not to worry for the rest of the journey home, which took hours and hours due to traffic. Poppy and I were reduced to doing the quizzes in her magazine again and pretending we didn't already know our scores.

AFTER AN ULTRASTRESSFUL WEEK BACK at school worrying incessantly about the postcard and dodging Mum's questions about how much I'd loved skiing, it appeared that I'd stumbled into a parallel universe! On Friday the postcard arrived and Poppy picked it up before anyone else in her house saw it! Poppy is usually so forgetful (like when she forgot how to spell the word "warm"—"walm, warlm, worm," then looked up her symptoms on the Internet and diagnosed herself with Mad Cow Disease). I hadn't been so relieved since my trousers split at the youth club and it turned out to be just a dream!

Then, on Friday afternoon Miss Rustford stopped halfway through the end-of-day register and said, "Sod it. Off you go. There's more to life than checking you lot are all here."

But . . . most importantly of all . . . the youth club finally got interesting!

I was really excited about seeing Luke after having been away skiing. Disappointingly, he sat in the front seat of the car because Poppy's mum didn't come along with us, but then he actually said hello to me! It was as if he was vaguely aware I hadn't been around for a while! It was brilliant. I decided I should talk to him about skiing but kept getting stuck while rehearsing the sentence in my head. If I told him I kept on falling over, wouldn't he just think I was a bit pathetic? I wished that I could study a textbook for situations like this, in order to avoid messing up. I ended up just smiling but not saying anything. Later on, though, the evening took a totally different turn.

"I must have scared Jez off with the postcard," said Poppy, looking worried when Jez didn't even look at her for the first hour. "I'll have to be less obvious."

"No, it'll just be because he's come with a friend," I

reassured her. "Typical Jez, he's just trying to look cool."

Jez was studiously ignoring Poppy in favor of doing mock karate kicks with his friend Charlie, who we hadn't met before. Charlie was quite short but good-looking. Later when he won against Jez in a round of table tennis, he flicked the ball at me! Poppy looked at me then widened her eyes wide suggestively in Charlie's direction.

"What?" I said.

"Nothing!"

Jez gave us a quizzical look, his first communication of the evening. We just looked back innocently.

At the end of the evening, everyone was forced through to the main hall for a quick kickabout (fantastic: football with rolled-up sweaters as goalposts). I was hanging back, thinking I could try to sit it out, when Charlie grabbed hold of my arm.

"Come on, let's get out of here," he said, gesturing toward the fire exit.

He opened the door. I glanced round at the last few people heading toward the main hall and followed him through to the car park. I leaned against the wall and looked up at the sky as the fire door clicked shut behind us and I took a deep breath, which helped fill the space left by not talking. I bet that's why some people smoke. Lighting a cigarette gives you something to do during awkward silences.

Suddenly, Charlie turned and put his arm around me!

"I could see you hesitating in there," he said, looking intently at me.

"Um—," I said. Was he implying that I'd been hanging back in order to be alone with him? It was more to do with an aversion to football.

"You're beautiful," he said unexpectedly—and before I could laugh or anything, he kissed me!

Oh my God.

It was all very interesting, of course. My First Kiss. But it was a bit sudden, and there was no music in my head or slow-motion looking-in-the-eyes first. (Not that it was ever going to be an idyllic moment, since we were outside a youth club in South London, not on a beach in California.) And I suppose I always thought it would be Luke. . . .

While I was considering this, Charlie stuck his tongue in my mouth! He rotated it vigorously as if he was trying to clean my teeth with his tongue. My overall impression was:

1. He didn't seem to care about my braces (good).
2. The kiss resembled someone sticking a wet, uninflated balloon in my mouth (not good).

All that stuff in books about it feeling really amazing didn't seem to be happening. When we stopped I didn't really know what to say. I wished I'd paid more attention to screen kisses on TV. Although at this point the scene usually ended in soft focus (not much help). I stepped back and hesitated, only to be interrupted by Poppy! She came outside and unsubtly cleared her throat.

"There you are! My dad's on his way."

Charlie put his hand on my arm and looked into my eyes.

"Why don't you put your number in my phone?" he said, handing me an incredibly tiny silver phone.

Well, why not? I keyed in my mobile number and almost handed it back, then remembered that my mobile phone was usually out of either battery or credit. Should I add my landline number as well? I typed it in but hesitated over the ENTER key. I didn't want Mum taking a call from a boy, but I didn't want to miss a call from Charlie either. And I was usually first to the phone while Ivy was at uni, so maybe it would be okay.

"You okay?" said Charlie, obviously wondering why I was staring, motionless, at his phone. I considered launching into a huge explanation but decided he would think I was mad.

"Fine," I said, hitting ENTER and handing it back. There was another pause.

"I'll put my numbers in your phone if you like," prompted Charlie.

Uh-oh. There was no way I was showing Charlie my rubbish old mobile! I had a brainwave and gave him something to write on instead. It was a shame that the only thing I had on me was my bus pass.

"I'll call you soon," Charlie said meaningfully before disappearing back inside.

In the car home Poppy's curiosity was unstoppable. "Did you *descendre avec . . .* him?"

"What?"

Poppy lowered her voice further, "Did you get off with him?"

Luke shot round from his position in the front seat. "What are you going on about?"

"Nothing," Poppy retorted. She turned back to me. "Did you?"

"Yes," I whispered.

Poppy's eyes widened. "What was it like?"

"It was *cool*."

She clearly couldn't decide what question to ask next, as what came out was, "What—where—how—tongues?"

"Tongues," I confirmed.

How annoying that this happened AFTER True Confessions!

I DECLINED A PLAYSTATION SESSION WITH Jamie on Saturday afternoon in order to lounge around the house all day playing love-struck music in my head. I felt very Adult and Experienced. I was just wondering if this meant that I was a strumpet too, like Claudia (no—one boy in one night is not bad; one is not like five), when Poppy called. She summoned me to an Emergency Snog Discussion Sleepover, which was brilliant. She asked about a billion questions about The Kiss. I told her how Charlie and I had talked in the moonlight and how he had brushed my hair gently away from my face before his lips met mine. Poppy seemed very impressed—though she did keep interrupting with details of what had happened with her and Yves. Which, though I didn't like to say, wasn't even a proper snog.

Poppy's mum complained on Sunday morning that she was kept awake by Poppy shouting "Goal!" We didn't tell her that she'd misheard—it was actually our new Snog-Measurement System that involved Poppy saying "Go!" and then me saying "Stop!" after mentally recalling how long Charlie and I had spent kissing (sixteen seconds). It was so cool. The previous week no one had fancied me. Now my love life was finally up to scratch! Also, at the back of my mind I suddenly felt more confident around Poppy. The kudos associated with having snogged someone had given me actual, real story material and instantly upped my coolness rating! Now I, too, exuded success with regard to the opposite sex.

Mind you, I had some questions:

1. How was I going to explain who Charlie was if Mum or Dad got to the phone first?
2. Was there any possibility Charlie would have grown by the next youth club?
3. Was a bus pass still valid if it had writing on it?

O N SUNDAY MORNING, AS SOON AS I got back home from Poppy's Emergency Snog Discussion Sleepover, I got out my Who-Likes-Who list and added Charlie. But what about the other name linked to mine? I couldn't exactly ask Poppy about it. It might damage my new, enhanced status, and anyway, she knew about as much as I did when it came to boys. So I did the obvious thing for real-life emergencies.

"Tell me everything!" Sasha yelled into the phone.

I went through it all (from under my duvet, surrounded by pillows for added secrecy), then said, "But that's not why I phoned. What about me and Luke?"

"Luke?"

"I still really like him. Isn't it wrong to go out with Charlie if I still like Luke?"

"Holly, you've hardly even spoken to Luke. You've snogged Charlie. With tongues!"

"Hmm."

Sasha sighed. "Maybe fancying Luke is like fancying a film star. It's . . . you know—unlikely to actually happen. And, well . . . he didn't even fancy Claudia, did he?"

I thought about it and decided she was right. There

must be something wrong with him. With Charlie, I had an actual boyfriend! Or, almost boyfriend. He hadn't actually phoned me yet, even though on Friday he had said, "I'll call you soon"! Was that bad?

I asked Sasha how it sounded, but she didn't know what "soon" meant, even when I repeated the whole sentence. We debated whether he might just text me, but Sasha made the valid observation that Charlie hadn't said "text," he'd said "call."

Then it occurred me that Charlie might be trying to get through, so we got off the phone.

Men Are From Mars, Women Are From Venus

I JUST CAN'T BELIEVE MY FAMILY SOMETIMES. On Thursday—almost a whole week after the kiss— the phone rang.

"Two margherita pizzas and a Coke," said a voice on the end of the phone. "Oh, and what Häagen-Dazs flavors do you have?"

"You've got the wrong number," I said, resisting the temptation to offer nutritional advice (eat healthily, though chocolate is clearly irresistible). I had just sat back down on the sofa when the phone rang again. I was back into the hall like a shot.

"WE DON'T SELL PIZZAS!" I enunciated very clearly, as if to a very small child.

"Holly?"

"Er, hi, Charlie."

99

"How come you haven't called me?" he said, wisely ignoring my deranged shouting.

"You haven't called *me*," I said huffily.

"I did. Yesterday. On this number. Your mum said she'd pass on the message."

What?

"Anyway, I just wondered if you wanted to go out tomorrow night?"

"Okay—cool!" I said. A date! As we arranged to meet up in town, all these thoughts whizzed round my head. How exciting . . . we could go to the cinema and he would put his arm round me and I would have a proper boyfriend! Mind you, I was also trying to recall the previous evening. I had phoned Sasha but that was all. Mum hadn't said Charlie had called! Had she kept it to herself because it was a boy? What if—

"I'll see you tomorrow, then," said Charlie.

"Sorry, I was just—," I said, but he had put the phone down.

Mum was in the kitchen trying to swat a fly with one of Dad's "Save the Wildlife" leaflets that she kept especially for the purpose.

"Mum, did anyone phone for me yesterday?"

She paused. Suddenly unpersecuted, the fly buzzed

joyously around a jar of peanut butter on the worktop. "Let me think." Mum wrinkled her nose in concentration and concluded, "No one phoned apart from Charlotte. I did call up to your room, you said you'd catch up with her at school in case the landline got clogged up." Mum resumed her athletic pursuit of the fly. "She was doing a silly voice."

Hang on a minute.

"Did she—what did she call herself?" I asked slowly.

Splat. Mum got the fly, which had been trying to fly through the window by repeatedly flinging itself against the glass.

"I don't know why you girls can't just use the lovely names you were given at birth," she said absentmindedly. "It's all 'Plop' this, 'Charlie' that. Their poor parents must despair."

Arrghh!

JUST OVER TWENTY-FOUR HOURS LATER, it was official. I had been on—and survived—my First Ever Date! Despite my mum having mistaken Charlie for a girl! And Charlie sent me a text on the way home afterward. I reread it so many times on the bus that I missed my stop. It said:

`Hi Hol—thx 4 2nite, Chaz X`

Was it just me or was that a bit short?

And—Chaz?

I supposed it was a bit like Jez, who is actually called Jeremy. However, I was not sure about the actual success of the evening. I decided to analyze it objectively in the back of my rough book:

Ideal Date

- Starts by being waved off by encouraging, modern mother.

- Boy suggests cinema. Accept graciously then sit in the dark, eating sweets and snogging.

Actual Date

- Translated date into Acceptable Mum Language, i.e. told her I was going to the youth club as usual.

- Accepted Charlie's suggestion of ice-skating at local indoor rink so he wouldn't think I was odd. Hid opinion that ice-skating is just pointlessly circling a big frozen disc of water, falling over regularly and possibly

	having your fingers chopped off by high-speed blades.
• Dazzle boy with brilliant conversation.	• Interrupted awkward silence by trying to ask about Charlie's hobbies, before screaming and falling over.
• Encounter people from school who look jealous.	• Encountered scary small children who laughed loudly at my skating skills.
• Meal in restaurant afterward (boy gallantly pays).	• Bus home afterward. No opportunity for gallant Charlie-paying due to ownership of (apparently valid) bus pass.

Disappointingly, there wasn't even a suitable time for any scandal once the ice-skating trauma was finally over and the important, saying-good-bye-and-passionately-snogging bit began. We talked for a bit and then suddenly my bus came!

"Did you enjoy tonight?" Charlie asked me while we made our way to the bus stop.

"It was brilliant!" I lied. It would be rude to tell him that I would have preferred the cinema.

"Really? I wasn't sure if you—"

"We should go again!" I interrupted cheerily.

"Uh—okay, I'll call you." Charlie looked unconvinced.

I thought I'd better check. "On my mobile? Or the landline?"

"Er—I don't know yet." Charlie looked a bit uncertain. "Is that a problem?"

Huh. The whole thing was Sasha's fault. She had been no help at all when I had told her I needed to figure out what to say in advance. She had just said I didn't need to!

"But I've never been on a date before!" I had told her. "Don't I need to prepare? You know, act interested in his hobbies and stuff?"

Sasha just said, "He's a boy, not a crap French pen pal."

How ironic that although Mum would have been thrilled that I had been ice-skating, I couldn't tell her! My double life was overwhelming; I know how Superman must have felt.

* * *

I SAW LUKE ON THE BUS THE FOLLOWING Wednesday and did think "yum" for an instant, but then remembered Sasha's wise words and suppressed the thought. It was obvious, really, that it was unlikely to actually happen. Anyway, I had Charlie now! Although, he hadn't actually phoned me since our date. One text message could only take a girl so far. Could his house be so big that he had misplaced his mobile? Should I phone him? I considered texting him (less scary), but I couldn't top up my phone credit until I got my pocket money on Saturday.

What I really needed were published guidelines about all this. It did occur to me that last year at school there was a presentation about a helpline called ChildLine, which was especially for young people to call for advice. Sasha called me so I asked her if she had a copy of the leaflet, but she reckoned ChildLine was mainly for if you were homeless or suicidal and stuff. Sasha also said I shouldn't phone Charlie, and if he phoned for me I should pretend to be out. It all sounded very complicated, especially given that Charlie *was* busy. He saw his dad every fortnight and visited his grandma once a week. It was amazing he had time to sleep, let alone have a love life! Then Sasha said,

"Anyway, I've got to be quick. I'm meeting Darren. I just needed to ask about spreadsheets." (Because she hadn't been listening during computing, not because she was suddenly interested.)

I briefly considered phoning Poppy for a second opinion, but she wouldn't know any more than me. Also, I was a teeny bit reluctant to ask her. She had been so interested and impressed since I got together with Charlie! I wanted her to think everything was fine. I had used to be able to say anything to Poppy, but since Claudia, I felt I needed to measure up—to be confident and know how to deal with stuff. So instead of calling her, I relied on a scientific, unbiased method of research. If my scrunched up bit of paper went in the bin then Charlie really fancied me and I should phone him.

SUCCESS! AFTER JUST A TINY BIT OF repositioning the bin! (Hmm. Perhaps I should play Goal Attack more often, rather than dawdling at the edge of the netball court in my Wing Attack bib.) However, covertly phoning a boy from the landline was no mean feat in my house. I had to sit for hours doing anagrams of people's names for English Language homework (Sasha Beresford spells "deaf brass horse" and Claudia Sheringham spells "I am a garlic he'd shun"—ha ha!). Finally, Mum decided to pop round to the neighbor's.

"I'm going to see Mrs. Heathfield," she said, before adding, "Dad is fixing Jamie's trampoline outside, so you're not by yourself, okay?" as if I would otherwise be tempted to graffiti the walls while she was out. "And when I get back we'll all be going out to Jamie's foot ball game."

I guessed I'd be going along too.

"See you later, alligator!" said Mum.

I looked at Mum impassively.

"In a while, crocodile," she finished off, unde-terred, and jogged out of the house in her lilac track-suit. No one in my family had any idea what was going on in my head. I would just go down to dinner as usual and listen to them going on about ten-mile hikes although everything had changed. How could they not tell? I felt like I might as well have had *I have snogged someone!* written on my forehead in big red capital let-ters with one of Jamie's felt-tip pens!

I crept into the hall and intrepidly dialed Charlie's

home number. (If I call mobiles from the landline, Mum wanders around with the itemized bill going, "Fifty pence a minute!" in an agonized tone.)

"Hello?" said a posh, cut-glass accent almost immediately.

"May I speak to Charles, please?" I said in my smartest voice.

"Who may I say is calling?"

"It's Holly." Why, did lots of girls phone him all the time? Charlie's mum sounded amused by me, Unknown Girl, phoning her son. Posh and amused was a fairly intimidating combination.

"Charleee! It's *Holly* for yoo-hoo!"

After a long pause, the phone clattered into life.

"Hello?"

"Hello. It's me, Holly. Erm—sorry. I was just calling to say hello."

Oh God, this was worse than a French oral. Why hadn't I written down something to say?

"Er—sorry, Holly. I can't talk now—my dinner's ready."

I was just thinking of something normal to add when I heard Mum's key in the front door and was forced to improvise.

"Okay, well, thanks for calling, Sasha! Bye!"

Oh dear.

But—mission accomplished—a conversation with my boyfriend!

The End of the Affair

WHAT I WANT TO KNOW IS THIS: HOW come one minute everything can be going fine and then suddenly life is a great big pile of elephant poo? Friday started off badly when Mrs. Mastiff somehow cottoned on to the fact that Jo and I were just walking along the bottom of the shallow end! I bet Susanna Forbes told her. Mrs. Mastiff made us join everyone else to do dives. Although deeply unpleasant, diving in is actually quite easy (just use gravity), but getting out of the deep end should be an Olympic sport in itself. Instead of gracefully levering myself out like everyone else I ended up sprawled, alongside the pool, like a Speedo-swimsuited twit.

I went over to Poppy's after school, relieved it was Friday, and we did the "Go!" "Stop!" thing again about

The Kiss (although I had to estimate. I couldn't even remember it properly the first time round, to be honest). Sasha called when I was walking back to my house and told me not to worry about the phone conversation with Charlie. Apparently boys only use the phone for arranging to meet people or for showing off, whereas girls see it as an extension of their very selves and have to be prized from it in order to eat, sleep, etc.

When I got home Jamie announced with a mischievous look toward the living room that a Boy Had Phoned for Me. Then, right on cue, Charlie called again!

"Hi!" I said like a twit, all confident since he'd phoned twice.

"Holly, we need to talk."

"Okay," I said hesitantly.

"I think we should just be friends."

Just friends? What that basically meant was "I don't want you to be my girlfriend"!

I couldn't think of anything to say so I shouted "Fine!" and slammed the phone down. In a dignified kind of way.

I knew it! I shouldn't have been allowed to deal with boys unaided, without a guide or a textbook. I knew I'd say something wrong! I wished I was seven again and still thought boys were just noisy, short-haired creatures who liked climbing things. It was all very . . . insulting.

POPPY AND I SPENT SATURDAY ON A shopping mission, so that I would forget about the Dumping Incident. On Friday night on the phone with Poppy, I had been a bit worried about telling her what had happened, in case my coolness rating plummeted. But she'd promptly come round, equipped for a sleepover with a shouty girl-power CD and some toffee popcorn! It was really sweet of her, especially because I knew she had been looking forward to seeing Jez at the youth club. Poppy listened to my reasoning and judged that it was doubtful that Charlie had dumped me because of my tangly hair since he hadn't been tall enough to run his fingers through it anyway. And ultimately how could Charlie have been rejecting me when he didn't even know me properly? Poppy is very wise.

Sasha called as well while Poppy and I were shopping so I told her what happened. She suggested

Charlie was overwhelmed by the enormity of his feelings for me and decided to end it because he was scared of getting hurt. Sasha is also very wise.

Anyway, I had to focus. Shopping is really complicated if you are a girl. It is simple for boys, who only have to choose between Large and Extra Large and never get told off for taking more than five items into the changing rooms. Poppy was going to buy a top in H&M but we didn't know if she wanted white, red, or black or if she was a size 38, 40, or 42, which gave nine possibilities. I just topped up my phone credit and bought a magazine (straightforward and only came in one size). Then Poppy dragged me to Boots to buy some pore strips for her nose. They are these sticky plasters which you put on, then peel off along with loads of blackheads and other gunk. Ugh.

"My nose is horrible close up," said Poppy. "It's no wonder Jez doesn't fancy me. And it's got a bump in it, if you look at it right. I'm really worried. What if it's some sort of bone disease?"

"He does fancy you," I said automatically, looking at where she was pointing. I couldn't see anything.

"No, he doesn't."

"Yes, he does."

Poppy gave me a yeah-right look.

"Why don't you just try asking him out?" I asked as we left Boots and headed toward McDonald's.

"What if he said no and it messed up us being friends?" said Poppy. "Why doesn't he ask me out? He's the boy."

Poppy and I reread Charlie's text in McDonald's. Poppy judged that it was all wrong ("no one kisses with a capital X"), bought me a strawberry milkshake, and told me Charlie was too short anyway.

Then in the evening Jez phoned my mobile and told me he'd just found out Charlie was two-timing me with some other girl called Chloë who was at boarding school in Brighton! Two-timing me! We were only going out for, like, five minutes! Jez said he thought I'd rather know what was going on. To be honest, I preferred Poppy and Sasha's interpretation of events.

"What does Chloë look like?" I asked Jez, perversely. Mum came into my room at that point under the pretense of hanging up school shirts, so I lowered my voice. "Is she pretty?"

Jez sounded bemused. "I haven't met her—does it matter?"

Does it matter? Boys were so weird sometimes, like they didn't realize anything. I bet she looked like Claudia. What if Charlie's visits to his grandma were just a front and he was actually seeing LOADS of girls? Grandma was an anagram of Amanda. Well, almost.

Oh my God. He was triple-timing Chloë and me with a girl called Amanda. What was wrong with Chloë and me? Weren't we enough for him?

CALLED POPPY ON SUNDAY MORNING AND went through it all in detail, but she didn't think Charlie would be bright enough to think of saying he was seeing his grandma if it was actually someone called Amanda. Maybe she was right that I was reading slightly too much into all this. But still. It called for a list:

SUMMARY OF MY LIFE

1. Poppy's parents can't drive us to the youth club next Friday because they are going out for their wedding anniversary. Which is just plain selfish.
2. I can't afford any of the clothes in the magazine I bought this weekend. *Funky in fuchsia!* says page

sixty, and then it has bright pink trousers for ninety pounds. Ninety pounds!

3. I bought two candy bars from the newsagent's earlier and he said, "Is this because of that boy who thinks you are weird?"

4. No one fancies me.

A millisecond after I got off the phone Mum appeared from the living room and said, "Come on, Holly—we're going to play rounders in the park." Either she moved very fast or she had been standing by the door, trying to listen in. Both were perfectly possible.

I thought about saying, "No, you crazed woman! That is the last thing I want to do. I am not joining in, and I won't ruin the house or get a tattoo if you leave me alone here for five minutes!" I contented myself with a sigh, which was enough for Mum to look at me with a familiar combination of mild irritation and dis-appointment. Usually this expression materialized when a family member chucked a ball in my direction and I simply leaned to one side and let the ball sail past instead of catching it. (Ah, the deadpan hilarity.)

Then Mum confused me by saying, "You know,

the word 'grandma' is almost an anagram of the word 'anagram.'"

I wish people would stop listening to my private conversations.

Persuasion

Y OU KNOW WHAT YOU NEED TO GET OVER
Charlie?" said Poppy during break the following Monday.

"Luke?" I said flippantly. Sasha had informed me
Charlie was just a practice snog and I had decided she
was right. I had just been trying to convince myself
he was a good idea when he wasn't, like when you see
great brown leather boots in the sale and try to ignore
the fact that they're only a size 3.

"I was going to say a holiday!" said Poppy.

"God, yes—like in our resolutions!"

"What's that?" said Claudia, interrupting as
she wandered past. "I'm going on holiday! To
Spain!"

"At Easter?" asked Poppy.

"No, in the summer. With Jo. One of those group ones. Dad was totally cool about it."

Unbelievable. Claudia could already go to her mum's villa in Sicily whenever she wanted and now her dad was paying for her to go on a Spanish beach holiday for teenagers! More to the point, I was immediately suspicious. Claudia had practically blanked Poppy for ages and now she wanted to talk to us again? Was she just materializing because Cool Tanya was otherwise engaged? (Year Ten was currently on a geography field trip in Wales.) Or was it just having a holiday to gloat about?

"It's fifty people, aged fourteen to eighteen, there's a Jacuzzi, AND it's mixed," said Claudia, reciting as many tempting statistics as possible.

"Mixed?" said Poppy. "Sounds brilliant!"

Hmm. What if Poppy and Claudia went on holiday together and left me at home dodging stray tennis balls?

"In fact," said Claudia meaningfully, "it's usually about seventy percent boys."

DON'T THINK MY PARENTS WANT ME TO have a life," I told Poppy on the bus the next morning as we looked at the brochure we'd borrowed from Claudia. We had started sitting upstairs every day, because Luke did. (It is amazing how many abandoned shoes you see on top of bus shelters. Do people have fights and throw the victim's shoes up there? How mean is that?)

Poppy sighed. "I was hoping yours would help convince mine."

She must have been joking! If Poppy's parents said no, there was no way I could convince mine. I pulled a face. "Bad news?"

"My dad said we weren't old enough to go away without them. It's not fair! Luke is the one that needs supervision. The other day I found him spraying deodorant on a fly." Poppy turned to scowl at Luke, sitting a few rows back. I turned as well so I would have a legitimate reason to look at him. Yum! Obviously I didn't want to scowl too but I couldn't smile either without diminishing the effect of Poppy's scowl. If you see what I mean. So he got a Blank Look instead, which probably looked unfriendly.

I was relieved that it was not just my parents that said no about the holiday. But still, it wasn't fair. I had timed my request so carefully! Dad had just finished watching golf, which meant he would be in a good mood, and Mum was reading *Badminton Monthly* on the sofa.

I had sat on the arm of the sofa and swung my legs. "Mum . . . ?"

"Ye-es?" Mum had said, obviously alerted by my tone that I wanted something. "I haven't got any chocolate."

Honestly. She hadn't even looked up.

"No, it's not that." I handed Mum the brochure. "There's this Spanish thing that everyone at school is going on."

"You just went skiing!" said Dad. "And you don't do Spanish."

"They've got activities and stuff. I could, um, learn diving."

There was a snort from Jamie in the corner.

"Hmm," said Mum, flicking through the pages "I'm not sure you're old enough. . . ."

Grr. "They are really well supervised."

"Aunty Valerie's son Paul wanted to go on one of these. They're very expensive. Is that a Jacuzzi in this picture?"

Huh! Mum's friend Aunty Valerie is the most boring, cost-conscious person alive. And how can she be a reliable source of information when she is not even a real aunty and we just have to call her that?

"It's really sporty, and I could pay you back?" I said hopefully, knowing that it wasn't, and I couldn't.

"I'm just not sure you're responsible enough to go away by yourself."

D'oh! "I would be with Poppy!"

"To be honest," Mum said, "that's not hugely reassuring. And anyway, it's very expensive. We're paying for your school's Own Clothes Day next week!"

I thought, honestly. That is one pound fifty.

"But . . ." I wanted to point out that they paid for me to go skiing when I hadn't even wanted to go! I didn't think that would help, though, so I kept quiet.

Mum gave Dad a Look and passed him the brochure.

"Look at these prices!" he said. He was no help at all. "I could buy a new set of golf clubs for that!"

They didn't seem impressed. My resolve weakened. I should have said: "Yes—but just think of the benefits of investing *in your own child*. Who can say thank you. Unlike a set of golf clubs!"

* * *

FTER HINTING ALL WEEK AT THE DINNER table ("In biology today we learned that sunshine aids the production of vitamin D!"), Mum told me to stop harassing her with the holiday brochure and said unreasonably that we were too poor and I was not old enough. Which were not negotiable, apparently. Poppy and I reluctantly progressed to discussing Own Clothes Day outfits instead. In our tragic purple and gray uniformed existence, the chance to wear whatever you like to school on the day you break up for Easter always tends to involve lots of discussion. Why do school uniforms exist, anyway? They are awful and serve no purpose at all. (Apart, Sasha says, from making you look ugly so boys don't fancy you so you do better in your exams.) I was originally going to wear my red top and my jeans, until I remembered everyone had seen them both on the skiing trip. So I decided that black combats and my dark blue vest top would be better. The decision became even more stressful when we heard that Claudia's dad had given her a hundred pounds to buy an outfit! I knew because Claudia had told Bethan and Bethan had told the whole of Year Nine.

Meanwhile, Sasha decided to wear her sister Jenny's new Levis. Jenny had left the labels on them to try to stop

Sasha from nicking them, but Sasha decided to simply borrow Charlotte's long cream jumper, which would cover the labels, then return the jeans undetected.

Rashida's mum was making her wear the sari that she wore to her cousin's wedding. Rashida had already hidden jeans and a Morgan top in a plastic bag in the locker rooms.

Poppy was having trouble with the decision as well. She asked me in the locker room, "Which pair of my jeans has the pockets in the most flattering position?"

"Um—they're all fine."

"I can't decide."

"Seriously. All fine. Or you could wear your three-quarter-length trousers instead?"

"I could do—yes!" Poppy looked momentarily inspired, then added, "But what if they just look like too-small trousers I've had since I was eight?"

"I know what you mean about three-quarter-length trousers," Claudia said to Poppy, emerging from nowhere. I fought the urge to climb into my locker and close the door. "I've got a pair of black trousers you can borrow if you like. They're really well cut—they would suit you."

"Thanks!" said Poppy. She looked surprised and pleased at once.

"Oh, and they're quite good for seduction," said Claudia matter-of-factly. "Huge success rate! I've been wearing them to and from tennis—it's only a matter of time with Greg."

I knew via Jo that Greg was Claudia's seventeen-year-old tennis coach. (Since summer term at Burlington's would soon involve a double whammy of swimming and tennis, Claudia's mum had bought Claudia advanced lessons. I think she'd also heard about Claudia's dad buying her the holiday in Spain.)

"I saw you wrote Greg's name on a desk in room 3B!" Poppy told Claudia, sounding keen.

Hmm. Hopefully Year Ten would soon be back from counting rocks, or whatever you do on geography field trips in Wales, then Claudia would disappear again.

ON THE LAST DAY OF TERM EVERYONE did the usual Easter thing of exchanging creme eggs and ending up with the same number they started out with. Oh, and turning up for Own Clothes Day in black boots (classic), black trousers (slimming), and white tops (go with black trousers). In math we told Mrs. Craignish it was wonderful not having to wear a school uniform. Mrs. Craignish said we must all feel very liberated.

As if chocolate eggs and no school uniform were not exciting enough, we had something new to talk about! Jez had called me the night before to tell me Charlie had been caught sneaking into Chloë's best friend's boarding-school window at three a.m.! I like Jez. Though, he had interrupted me mid-ponder about whether I should wear my stretchy black dress. (I decided against it in the end. If you wear what is clearly your best outfit, it looks as if you consider Own Clothes Day the most interesting thing that will happen to you all year.)

Poppy and I discussed the Jez conversation in detail at lunchtime while we were preparing our tennis racquets for next term (using Claudia's Tippex to cover the scratched bits).

"Who's Charlie?" said Claudia.

"Holly's ex-boyfriend," said Poppy.

"Really?" said Claudia, looking mildly impressed. "How did you meet him?"

"Friend of Jez's," I said.

"And now he's an ex?"

"He was really short," I said, giving a vague question a vague answer. Poppy gave me a Look. I gave her a Look back that said, *Well, he was!*

"So—Poppy, are you going out with Jez yet, then?" said Claudia.

"No," said Poppy. "But I'll see him at the youth club tonight."

"I can't believe you have known each other for so long and nothing has happened!"

I blew on my tennis racquet to dry the patches and said nothing. "You okay?" asked Poppy a few minutes later.

"Fine," I said. Of course I didn't mind if Poppy had other friends. I mean, we both did—I was friends with Sasha, and Poppy didn't mind. But that was different. With Poppy and Sasha it was never a case of replacing one with the other, they just had different bits of my life. And although we both got on really well, Sasha mainly had her own gang of friends outside school. But with Claudia it felt as if she was after the same territory as me. And more to the point, Poppy seemed to get wrapped up in this exciting new friendship! Last time, with the whole Luke thing, she had seemed to enjoy leaving me out and hitting me where it hurt with the suggestion that Claudia and Luke would get together. Maybe it had gone too far and Poppy hadn't meant for it to happen. But she had never said sorry, had she? What if she just did it again?

THE EASTER HOLIDAYS ALWAYS MAKE IT clear to me that I, Holly Stockwell, live in a boring house on a boring street where gorgeous boys stay in their boring houses and don't walk past often enough. After a few days I had watched every DVD I owned, read all my books, and eaten all my Easter eggs. And how were we supposed to have illicit parties when no one's parents had gone away?

Oh, and even by the very last weekend of the Easter holidays, Mum wasn't giving up on "getting me moving."

"Ivy and I are going to do an aerobics DVD in a minute," she told me on Saturday. "Do you fancy it? You've been reading in your room all day!"

That was clearly inaccurate, since I was standing in the kitchen quietly boiling the kettle for a hot chocolate. Okay, I'd been in my room until then, but what did she expect? Ivy was back from uni with all these brand-new monologues about nightmarish sports teams!

"I'm going over to Poppy's later," I said in my defense.

"What, so you'll sit in her room instead?"

Mum is so overzealous sometimes. I walk lots every day and it is not as if I am fat or anything (with the possible exception of my bottom). In fact, I am one hundred percent normal with just a teeny, tiny bit of restfulness thrown in. Just because the rest of my family takes sport to extremes, I am supposed to do the same!

"You know, you'd enjoy joining a team, doing something competitive," Mum continued, wrongly. "The tennis club meets on Saturday! You look so serious when you've been cooped up."

"It's not that," I said. Actually, the Poppy and Claudia thing had been on my mind. It sounds really pathetic, but suddenly I wanted a mum I could really talk to about stuff like this. Friends. And boys, come to that—without the ensuing surveillance.

"It's just this thing. . . . Someone's going off with one of my friends," I said, avoiding eye contact. I added hastily, "Just now and again," before she ran to the library in a panic for a book about counseling friendless teenage offspring.

"Are they leaving you out?"

"Not exactly. We're all talking and stuff. It's just . . . they've left me out before. It's horrible. I used to be the one—you know—who was involved in stuff," I reached up and got the hot chocolate powder from the cupboard. "It makes me feel like my friend isn't really my friend. That I'm not important to her."

Mum picked up the kettle as it clicked off. "Holly. Don't let it bother you. You can't stop someone being friends with other people. You're still her friend too, aren't you?" She spooned some of the powder into my favorite stripy, oversize mug.

"I know," I said sulkily, watching Mum pour boiling water into the cup and press out the lumps with the back of a teaspoon. I had realized that; I wasn't totally stupid. But it still changed everything.

"Just try joining in. Some friends come and go and some are there for life. Like . . . I don't know . . ." Mum handed me my drink and stared at the mugs in the kitchen cupboard. "Like plastic beakers compared to china cups."

That was quite sweet, in an odd way. Mum has friends she's known since she was at school, I guess. But what if I was a plastic beaker?

Dangerous Liaisons

WHAT WOULD YOU RATHER . . . ," began Poppy with visible relish. Claudia, Poppy, and I were settled in Poppy's bedroom in front of *American Beauty* (DVD player pinched from the living room and DVD pinched from Luke's room while he was out at Craig's).

Yes, Poppy, me, and Claudia.

The thing is, Poppy had invited me to sleep over, which saved me from writing *BORED* all over my tiny boxroom walls in lipstick. It was just the two of us to start with, but while we were sat on her bed reading our horoscopes, Claudia phoned! I tried not to sulk too visibly.

Poppy promptly hit END CALL. "Claudia's coming round too."

"How come?" I examined a hole in my sock.

"To talk about me and Jez. You don't mind, do you?"

Maybe I should have gone home on grounds of intense dislike for Claudia, but I didn't want to risk Claudia going off with Poppy again, or anything happening with her and Luke. So I stayed.

Something gave me the impression Poppy wasn't really watching *American Beauty*. Perhaps it was the way she was bouncing up and down and gleefully repeating, "What would you rather?" She had clearly been preparing this one while Claudia had been going on about Greg. (I had been keeping quiet, trying to assess my plastic-beakeriness.)

Poppy finally finished her sentence. " . . . eat this toenail clipping that I just found on my floor, or get the bus to school naked?"

"I'd have to . . . eat the toenail," I said, adding lightly, "it might be one of Luke's!"

I glanced at Claudia to gauge her reaction, but got none. She was just brushing her hair with a big pink brush.

"Uuuugggghhhhh!" Poppy wrinkled her nose. "That's grim."

"I'd get the bus naked!" pronounced Claudia, her voice muffled from bending forward to brush her hair. She flicked it back and smiled confidently at us both. "That would give everyone something to stare at!"

It was my turn now. "Who would you rather snog—an eleven-year-old boy or Miss Rustford?"

"Ugh!" said Poppy, throwing the toenail clipping at me in disgust. I dodged it.

"It would have to be Miss Rustford," said Claudia, remarkably calm considering what she was saying. "I couldn't kiss an eleven-year-old boy."

"Not even that one who bought you the Valentine's card?" Poppy asked.

"No way. I just let him down gently."

Poppy nodded wisely and said, "Yeah, I had to do that with Yves." I couldn't resist a "pah!" noise. Poppy ignored me and said to Claudia, "Holly's not had anyone to let down gently!"

She said it jokily, just in a teasing way, but I thought to myself, Oh, thanks a lot!

When it was Claudia's turn at What Would You Rather, she changed the subject, for which I was pretty grateful. "About you and Jez," she said to Poppy. "I am going to help you two get together properly."

Poppy made an I'm-not-sure face. "I'm not sure," she said, right on cue. "We get on quite well at the moment. I want to just leave it and see what happens."

"If you leave it to boys, nothing will ever happen. What have you done so far?"

"I wrote him a postcard from skiing."

"And what happened?"

"Nothing."

"Then you need to engineer it." Claudia looked at me and smiled. "Holly, will you tell her? She needs to get on with it!"

What did I know? But Claudia seemed to think my opinion mattered here!

"Uh—yes, she's right," I said.

Poppy looked bashful. "But—"

"Like me and Greg!" interrupted Claudia. "Or Holly and, uh, Carl—"

"Charlie."

"Sorry, like Holly and Charlie," Claudia said. She turned to look at me again. "Holly, I meant to say, I never knew you had had a boyfriend before!"

"It's a miracle, isn't it?" I said, before I could help myself.

Claudia giggled. "Don't be ridiculous, you're really

pretty. I mean, you never mentioned it! I guess we just haven't had the chance to talk properly before now."

"No," I said, half flattered and half suspicious. I thought, Well, why haven't we talked before now? Oh yes, because earlier this year you were busy stealing my best friend and the love of my life, and I was busy thinking you were the devil incarnate. Perhaps now that Claudia had Greg, she was in friend-hunting rather than man-hunting mode? Though, she did sound genuinely interested. Really I should have corrected her and explained that Charlie had hardly been a full-on boyfriend, and that he had dumped me after about five minutes! But, the funny thing was, it was enjoyable being thought of as cool and experienced for a change.

"Anyway, sorry, Poppy. I was saying, you just need to know how to hook them!" said Claudia, back to the topic of Jez. She was like a whirlwind, dashing about from one thing to the next. "There are LOADS of things you could do. Invite him swimming so he sees you in a bikini. Or go ice-skating and make him catch you by accidentally falling over—"

"Falling over?" I said faintly.

"Yes, falling over," said Claudia more loudly this

time, obviously considering that my hearing was the issue.

"Isn't that a bit . . . obvious?" said Poppy. But she sounded almost intrigued.

"You have to be obvious with boys or they just don't notice."

Poppy looked worriedly at her fingernails. "Is there anything just slightly more subtle?"

"Well, you could arrange a cinema trip," said Claudia as if this was the easiest thing in the world. "And go in the afternoon, not the evening, if you want to make it seem as if it isn't a date. Even better, invite a group. Ask some of his friends as well. And we'll come, won't we, Holly?"

Hurrah! Suddenly I didn't want to miss out.

Poppy hesitated, "I don't know."

I stared at the television, where a plastic bag was blowing around on the screen. I could offer to phone Jez. But to be honest I agreed with Poppy. Just casually asking him to the cinema? Scary!

"I'll do it," said Claudia. "When we're back at school. I'll arrange it for you."

"Okay, then," said Poppy, looking relieved. "Why not?"

I tried unsuccessfully to get Mouse to run through a 100 roll tube, feeling a bit uncertain. Where was all this going? Okay, we were all here together at the moment, actually having—dare I say it—quite a fun night. But was Claudia only including me because I was there? You know, being nice because the situation demanded it? Where would I be in a week or two? Part of a secure, happy friendship? Or sitting on the sidelines?

CLAUDIA WAS TRUE TO HER WORD. ON Monday lunchtime at school she phoned Jez, introduced herself, and arranged for us all to go out that weekend! It was pretty impressive. What was even more notable was that Miss Rustford walked past, saw Claudia's illicit mobile phone, and didn't say anything! But this was eclipsed on Thursday by even more Boy News. Claudia ran up to us in the playground before registration. "Had tennis last night," she said, "but . . . I didn't get much practice done!"

Poppy gasped. "You and Greg got together?"

"He told me he dumped his girlfriend and she cried," Claudia said proudly. "She's doing her A-levels this year. But apparently he's fancied me for ages!"

Claudia was interrupted by her phone ringing. She answered it.

"It's Jez," said Claudia to Poppy. "He wants to speak to you."

Poppy listened intently for a moment, then said, "Holly, Jez says he's bringing his cousin Stuart to the cinema for you."

"What? Give me the phone."

"Holly wants a word," Poppy hastily told Jez.

"I'm not going near any more moldy friends of yours after Charlie!" I exclaimed into the handset. Poppy and Claudia fell about laughing, which was very pleasing. It was much easier to be bold with boys when it was Jez, who was Poppy's and therefore didn't count.

"Claudia said she wanted there to be a group of us," protested Jez smoothly. "That is, unless you . . . well, Stu is really good-looking. He's my cousin. Tall. Blond hair. You would like him."

"Why me? Why not Claudia?"

"She mentioned she fancies some bloke called Greg. She doesn't need a date. I mean, not that you do—"

"I only like boys with dark, curly hair and green eyes," I said firmly, just to be on the safe side. However I was quietly pleased because now I was not the Ugly Friend who had no one to go to the cinema with!

We let Claudia figure out our seating plan for the cinema in math, using Poppy's desk as a strategy board and scrunched-up bits of rough book to represent different people.

"Who's this?" whispered Sasha, leaning over. She pointed at a ball of paper and looked at me. I could tell that what she actually meant was, "Why are you planning something with Claudia?"

"That's Poppy," I said firmly. "She's going to sit here, next to Jez. In the back row."

"Then Claudia or Holly will sit next to me," said Poppy, "so it won't look too artificial." She looked at Claudia, who smiled in approval. I was looking forward to it. Finally, an Actual Boy Mission, planned by an expert!

"And so," I said, pointing at the final two balls of paper, "Jez's cousin Stu can sit next to me—but only if he's nice—and—most importantly—Poppy can get to snog Jez."

Simple! Now we just had to speed up/slow down at the right moments to achieve this seating plan, without it being at all obvious to the boys.

Sasha looked at the bits of paper and asked the question that had been at the back of my mind since Claudia had breezed back into our lives.

"What, no Luke?"

I could have hugged her. But Claudia just laughed!

"Luke?" she said. "He's gorgeous—honestly—but he's not my type. No offense, Poppy, but he's just so reserved! Greg is really outgoing."

I looked carefully at Claudia, but all I saw was genuine loved-up-ness.

Unexpectedly, I felt quite fond of her.

I think Mrs. Craignish could tell we weren't doing percentages, but she was quite relaxed about it. She walked past our desks at one point and said, "I remember when the only complication was getting stuck behind someone tall!"

I FELT REALLY INVIGORATED BY CLAUDIA'S expert planning. It was enjoyable being along for the ride. Plus, she knew so much stuff! Although, was the fact that Luke was "reserved" good or bad? I couldn't tell.

Sasha called that night to ask about the percentages

for math homework. I looked them up in the back of the book for her since I hadn't actually been listening either, then she said, "So, Claudia's back, then?"

"She's helping matchmake Poppy and Jez."

"Not just bored?"

Why did Sasha always have to be so acidic?

"Actually, she's being really nice at the moment!" I said. "She's sweet once you get to know her a bit. It's impressive—she's really enthusiastic about stuff and isn't scared to ask boys out. Actually, she reminds me a bit of you!"

"Really?" said Sasha, a touch icily. Oh dear I had spoken without fully thinking about what was coming out of my mouth.

"Sorry," I said, making a mental note that people who seemed similar wouldn't necessarily be delighted to hear about it.

Fortunately, Sasha let it go. "So, you're a new Claudia fan! You've changed your tune!"

If I went right to the back of my mind, I was still scared Poppy and Claudia could drop me at any minute. But things were going really well!

"I think I was just being jealous."

"No you weren't, they were really mean to you,"

said Sasha, making a little sucking noise with her teeth.

"I'd rather not bring all that up again," I said, wishing we'd stuck to the subject of percentages. "And I don't think they're going to do it again. It doesn't feel like it."

"You shouldn't have to worry about your friends ganging up on you, though. You should *know* they won't!"

But I couldn't know for sure, could I? That would involve going into the whole awkward subject with Poppy, and probably messing things up. Anyway, Poppy and Jez should have gotten together ages ago. I didn't feel like a plastic beaker. What was wrong with the *three* of us being friends?

After getting off the phone, I made a new, radical list:

GOOD THINGS ABOUT CLAUDIA

1. She is getting Poppy and Jez together.
2. She is very determined and bold about things, especially boys.
3. She lent us her Tippex.

And maybe if I asked nicely, Claudia would let me go and live in her poolhouse or garage or something, in order to get some privacy from my family? Mum wandered randomly into my room while I was finishing the Claudia list and started rabbiting about me making friends with some girl in Year Eleven! Apparently she was called Lorraine, had just moved in across the street, and was now going to Burlington's too. But since when did girls from Year Eleven talk to girls from Year Nine?

"Do I have to?" I asked Mum.

Mum seemed genuinely oblivious to the fact that both Lorraine and I would probably rather eat our own earwax.

"Well, no, but you should. Just think—you'll be able to just pop across the street and have a nice chat. A new friend just across the road!"

Ah, I see. I knew it was odd that this new idea hadn't involved any competition or physical pain. She was trying to find me some new friends after I had foolishly mentioned the Claudia issue! She needn't have worried. To prove my qualms had been unfounded, I told Mum about the cinema. You know, how it was just going to be me, Poppy, and Claudia.

"Who's Claudia?" she asked, as if Claudia was a drug dealer, or worse, a boy.

"Poppy's friend. With the dark hair."

"Oh, yes—Vanessa Sheringham's daughter! The pretty girl. What rating is the film?"

"Don't worry, it's only a Twelve." I refrained from adding, "But we are planning some very unsuitable Advanced Snogging in the back row."

"I don't want you girls coming back late on the bus."

"It's only in the afternoon!"

"Okay. Well, as long as you take your phone."

Women in Love

FINALLY CINEMA DAY ARRIVED. WHEN WE met up early at Poppy's, Claudia promptly produced two tops from her bag!

"A present," she said, throwing a lovely white halterneck toward Poppy and a black vest top toward me.

"Are you sure?" we said in unison. Poppy held up her top and looked at Claudia.

"Of course! Try it on—it will really suit you."

Poppy looked a bit uncertain but put it on. She liked her clothes quite comfy and casual whereas the halterneck fitted really closely.

"It's gorgeous," I said. She looked great. And the top Claudia had given me was so nice. It felt like my birthday or something! We got changed while Claudia frowned at Poppy's collection of jeans. Finally,

Claudia found a black skirt at the back of Poppy's wardrobe. Poppy protested that her mum had bought it. Claudia said it was perfect.

When we turned up outside the cinema (fashionably late, at Claudia's insistence), Jez was there waiting. So was his friend Mohammed! Poppy, Claudia, and I all exchanged looks. Mohammed was very nice, but he wasn't part of the Seating Plan. Also, Jez and Mohammed were accompanied by a tall bloke with mad-looking blond eyebrows and eyelashes.

"Hi," said Jez. He looked at Poppy for longer than strictly necessary but failed to tell her she looked nice! Claudia rolled her eyes at me. I rolled mine back. It was amusing having a mutual mission.

"This is Stu," continued Jez, confirming my fears by pointing at Eyebrow Boy.

Stu nodded hello and studied my chest with clear disappointment. I am not as well endowed as Claudia, who hasn't been able to see her own feet since she was twelve. I glared at Jez, who pretended not to notice.

The plan was for Poppy to get to sit next to Jez, but getting to our seats became a game of wits hidden under a veneer of nonchalance. I walked quickly to avoid Stu-the-Chest-Starer, but he caught up with me, so I stopped to wait for Poppy, who was farther back (carefully walking at the same pace as Jez). But in the darkness of the cinema it all went wrong and Poppy ended up walking just behind Mohammed, who sat down randomly without even having had the good sense to pick the back row! Then Stu followed directly behind Poppy. Poppy looked helplessly toward me. I tried to save the situation by putting my hand on Stu's arm to slow him down, but this only made him grin suggestively. With the air of somebody who was watching a history program when expecting entertainment news, Poppy edged along the row and sat down reluctantly next to Mohammed. Stu followed Poppy in, as if he didn't realize *anything*. Was he mad? I looked round to see if Jez or Claudia could at least sit next to him, but Jez was holding Claudia's popcorn while she tied her shoelace. I had no choice but to follow Stu. We all sat down in silence. Poppy leaned over Stu to pass the pick-and-mix candy, and pulled a small, private "Oh God" face. I did an "I know" face in return. Not good. No one got to sit next to the right person, and not even squares of vanilla fudge could ease the pain!

* * *

ESPITE THE LACK OF SNOGGING DURING the cinema trip, I had to be impressed by the success of Claudia's plan so far. I could tell things had moved along because Jez and Poppy started flirting at the youth club. Well, marginally. They would get chips together from the snack machine on the other side of the room then return deep in conversation.

"One day," Jez said on one occasion as they headed back over with a packet of Hula Hoops each, "we should both bunk off school and meet up in London."

"Like in that film—*Ferris Bueller's Day Off*!" I contributed. "But London, not Chicago."

"That would be cool," said Poppy.

"We should do it," Jez said, looking just at Poppy, who promptly looked as if she might faint. I quickly moved next to her in case she needed holding up.

WAS NOT MAKING SIMILAR PROGRESS WITH Luke. On the way home from the youth club one night, I managed to walk next to Luke toward the car! My arm brushed against his arm three times! Unfortunately he noticed and said, "Are you okay, Holly?" I knew I had to say something but I couldn't think of anything convincing. (A minor medical condition that meant I couldn't walk straight? There must be one. I should pay more attention to Poppy's medical research.) So I just said, "Fine."

Anyway, by early May, Jez was calling Poppy almost every day! It was usually when we were on the bus home from school. Poppy would put her mobile on speakerphone, and then we'd call Claudia afterward to update her.

"The next step is to get invited over to his house during half term," advised Claudia from Matchmaking Headquarters (her bedroom in Lansdowne) after the latest call. "You really need to hike things up a notch."

"Could you—," said Poppy.

"Don't worry!" said Claudia. "I'll call him and hint a bit for you, if you like."

Poppy nodded, before obviously remembering Claudia couldn't see her and instead saying, "Thanks Claudia!"

She hit END CALL and I was about to speak when Luke came up the bus stairs! He was holding an HMV bag, which explained why he was getting on the bus by the shops instead of by his school. Poppy and I were sitting on one pair of seats each (we could still talk but it looked cooler than sitting together) and—wait for it—Luke sat next to me! Even though there was a free seat next to Poppy!

"I'm not sitting next to her," Luke said in greeting. "She smells."

I grinned out of sheer surprise, before realizing that smiling at this was probably a bit disloyal. At the same moment I remembered my braces and shut my mouth firmly.

"You pig!" said Poppy, hitting him across the back of the head.

"Are you like this with your brother and sister?" said Luke, leaning toward me to shield himself from future blows.

The combination of him sitting so close and talking directly to me was a bit overwhelming. Actually I wasn't even aware he knew I had a brother and sister, but he had obviously picked it up somehow. I felt the magnitude of my task bear down on me. How was I going to impress him? What was the best thing to say?

"Uh—no," I squeaked. Unfortunately at that moment Jamie rang me. I think the ringtone was supposed to be *Star Wars*, but it had clearly been composed in under a minute with no real care.

"Oh God!" I said, reaching into my bag and hitting END CALL.

Luke looked at me quizzically and raised an eyebrow. The effect was devastatingly sexy. I held on to the bus seat with one hand so I wouldn't fling myself at him.

"It's just my brother, Jamie," I said, speaking way too quickly.

"He's only eleven," said Poppy, by way of explanation. "He does that to wind her up."

"Was it him who did *Postman Pat*?" Luke asked me. I'd forgotten about that. "Oh—yes!"

"Do you ever answer him?"

"Um—no. No, I don't." God! Why was I only able to talk in monosyllables instead of witty sentences? I was just trying desperately to think of an amusing *Postman Pat*–related comment (not easy) when my phone rang again. This time, it was Mum. What?! Could she tell I was sort of talking to a boy? Did she have cameras installed on the bus or something?

"Are you nearly home? We're going out to play squash."

"Right," I said cautiously, not committing myself.

"We'll wait for you, so you can come with us," said

Mum firmly and put the phone down. (She is Very Concerned about the Cost of Mobile Phone Calls.)

I turned to get back to Luke, suddenly inspired. I'll ask what he's bought from HMV! But he was chatting on his phone.

OKAY, THE PLAN WAS DEFINITELY working. Jez invited me, Poppy, and Claudia over to his house on the last Friday of half term, when his parents would be away! He would never have done that at the start of the year! We even convinced him to refrain from producing any more dodgy friends. My only concern was that Mum was the one driving us to his house, because Poppy's parents were busy. I might have implied that it was a girl called Jessica's house, her parents were going to be there, and they would be happiest if Mum just dropped us at the end of the street.

Poppy was thrilled and couldn't concentrate on anything at all after Jez called. During French on the last day before half term she whispered to Claudia, "So, during your tennis lessons, do you play with Greg's balls?"

"Do the two of you make a racket?" I added.

Poppy groaned. Claudia looked up from idly polishing her DKNY watch. "Dumped Greg."

"What?" I said.

"I dumped Greg. Yesterday."

Miss Rustford turned round. "Everything okay?"

"Fine," we chorused automatically. We were supposed to be working in small groups and describing our houses, but we had decided we already knew what they were like.

"Well, as long as you are prepared by exam time," said Miss Rustford in a relaxed manner and went back to her marking.

I was surprised about Greg—Claudia had really seemed to like him. However, yet again her whirlwind enthusiasm had disappeared as quickly as it had started. Claudia ripped a page agonizingly slowly from her rough book so it wouldn't make a noise, then scribbled a note: *Greg more interested in his PlayStation than in me. Told parents got bored of tennis.*

All the *i*'s on the note were topped with little hearts as normal. I could hardly believe it—she really was unbothered by everything. Practically superhuman!

A la Recherche du Temps Perdu

BEFORE I KNEW IT, MOST OF HALF TERM had gone! I had resolved to be much more organized than ever before and to revise in advance for June's end-of-year exams. That way I could spend the second half of the week's holiday relaxing, planning deceptive visits to boys' houses, etc. But by Friday, although I had revised, somehow it didn't feel as if I had done enough. Not that it was all my fault:

DANGEROUS DISTRACTIONS FROM REVISING

1. Enhancing revision chart with color-coding systems, different keys with the topics to be studied, and little star-shaped stickers to indicate hours of work completed.

2. Borrowing Jamie's keyboard (leaving the window open while playing in case I discovered a hidden talent for music and Luke walked past and thought I was really good).
3. People-watching from window.
4. Thinking about Mum driving us to Jessica's on Friday. What if Mum insisted on coming in and talking to Jessica's parents? She was bound to notice then that they didn't exist. Or Jessica.

I had just decided to ban lists of distractions (for being distracting) when the phone rang. It was Poppy, inviting me to get ready for Jez's round at her house. Officially it clashed with the French oral practice scheduled on my revision chart, but Poppy said, "Oh, come on, Holly, your French is already really good. You worry about it far too much. Even your mum thinks you should revise less!"

"Only because she thinks sports are more important. You don't get medals for passing exams. And my French isn't that good! I need to do loads of revision for the oral. They really put you on the spot."

"French is easy," said Poppy. "All you have to do is say, 'Er . . .' in a French accent and wave your arms about. If it all goes wrong, blame Miss Rustford. It's her who's failed to nurture your talent by forcing you to learn stupid verbs."

What? Had she been talking to Sasha or something? "I still need to learn loads of vocab, though," I protested.

"Look, come over and we can do What Would You Rather in French while we're getting ready. Claudia's coming over too."

So I went.

AFTER A LOT OF PREPARATION AT POPPY'S (which didn't involve any What Would You Rather in French, as we didn't know the vocab for "snogging" or "vomit") we made it over to Jez's.

Jez's house was really posh, with a grandfather clock and deep pile cream carpet. The members of his family had a bathroom *each*! There was one upstairs, a shower room under the stairs, and another in his parents' bedroom. I know this because Jez gave us a tour.

I think Jez had been getting bored in the house by himself. He hadn't quite got round to revising either by the look of things. He claimed he had a headache after raiding his parents' drinks cabinet with Charlie the night before. "I took a bit from each bottle and drank it all mixed together," Jez explained.

Poppy looked doubtful. "Was it nice?"

Jez shrugged as he disappeared into the kitchen. From the hall, I could see a big pile of washing up and empty pizza boxes. "It was, you know, alcoholic," he said with the air of One Experienced in the Ways of Drinking.

"My parents never let me stay in the house on my own," I commented.

Claudia looked surprised. "Really? Never?"

"Never!" Not even for five minutes, if Mum could help it.

"My neighbor comes in every day," said Jez. "To check I haven't driven off in Dad's BMW."

"My mum's always out at work or with her boyfriend," said Claudia. "So basically I can do what I want!"

Blimey. She is so lucky.

Poppy and I went into the living room and sat down in an armchair each. Bizarrely, I felt nervous on Poppy's behalf, while she seemed perfectly at ease.

Ironically, being at ease with Jez was partly Poppy's problem. She could quite merrily see him for ages without being bold enough to make the move beyond friendship. Claudia was equally relaxed, as if she'd been to Jez's hundreds of times before. She sat on the cream leather sofa and stretched her legs out across the cushions, heels and all, so when Jez came in the room holding drinks he had to hover for a moment.

"Sorry, am I in your seat?" said Claudia, moving her legs.

"No problem." Jez handed out the drinks and sat down next to her. "Shall we watch a DVD?"

It was brilliant watching a film on their big TV with surround sound and the lights dimmed—like being at the cinema. I kept thinking how Luke would love it. I looked over a few times at Claudia, thinking she might need to catch my eye to engineer leaving Jez and Poppy alone together, but she didn't see me.

After the film, Claudia went to get a Coke. Aha! I got up and was about to make an excuse to join her, but before I could leave, she reappeared in the doorway of the lounge holding a football shirt.

"Is this yours?" she asked Jez. "It was on the line in your utility room. Can I try it on?"

"Why?"

"I love Arsenal. I used to go to matches with my dad!" Claudia pulled it on over her T-shirt. I was just thinking how well the color suited her when the doorbell rang. Five minutes early! I looked at Poppy, who had the stricken air of Cinderella finding that midnight had been rescheduled for five minutes to ten. I peered round the living room door and saw my mum, rippled through the frosted glass in her pale yellow tracksuit! Two things went through my mind: yellow tracksuit—why? And couldn't she have just waited at the end of the street like I had asked her to?

"Will your mum be here in a minute?" Poppy asked Claudia.

"What—my mum drive all the way here to pick me up?" said Claudia. "No way, she'll call me a cab. But I thought we said eleven?"

"Ten," said Poppy

"Oh." Claudia looked as if she didn't know what to say. "Sorry, I got it wrong."

"You could call the cab firm?" I suggested.

"I haven't got their number in my phone."

Meanwhile, Jez had gone out into the hall to open the door. Honestly.

"Get back here!" I hissed at Jez. "My mum thinks this is Jessica's house!"

I ran into the hall and pushed a protesting Jez into the bathroom under the stairs. Thank God for extra bathrooms.

"Who's Jessica?" said Claudia.

"Yes, who's Jessica?" echoed Jez plaintively, his voice muffled from inside the bathroom.

"Never mind," I said, as Poppy walked over and opened the front door. Poppy cleared her throat loudly to mask the indistinct thumping noise from the bathroom. We all smiled innocently.

"Did you have a nice time?" said Mum. "Where's Jessica?"

"Bathroom," I said, exiting hastily.

"We had a great time, didn't we?" said Poppy. I glared at her, but Poppy just kept grinning like a nutter and saying mischievously, "Yes, Jessica's really, really nice!"

A S SOON AS WE WERE BACK AT SCHOOL, Poppy's mum told Poppy there would be no more going out until after the exams. This was hugely unfair—Poppy and Jez were just getting warmed up, plus no more youth club meant no Luke-watching! Of course, it was suddenly really sunny every day—typical, sadistic English weather. At lunchtimes the whole of Year Nine started sitting outside in the playground with their skirts around their thighs and their socks pulled down, while comparing tan lines left by their watches. A few times I even saw that Year Eleven girl, Lorraine, that my mum had mentioned. She has dyed red hair and looks a bit scary.

Everyone in Year Nine occupied themselves with revision conversations, which all go something like this:

Person A: I haven't done any work! Help!

Person B: I really haven't done any. I'm not just saying that.

Person A: No, I mean it. Honestly. I haven't even opened the book.

Person B: I don't know any of it! I am badly going to fail.

Mind you, nobody actually meant it, apart from me. I was really worried. What if I failed every exam?

What if I'd revised the wrong bits? I couldn't have learned everything. Some of the handwriting in my exercise books was impossible to read where I had obviously fallen asleep during the lesson! What if the exams were on those bits?

Then, when the exams actually started, it was just as bad as I had thought. The stress was even getting to Sasha, who was freaking out about the typing test in the computing exam and kept claiming that she was going to cheat by turning on the automatic spell checker. The science exam alone took about five years off my life expectancy. Teachers get so scary and official in exams, pacing the room, staring at your answers, and making you jump by announcing things like "You may start!" and "Five minutes left!" I reckon they only do it to make everyone more nervous.

"God, that was *awful*," Sasha said as we were leaving the science room.

"What was the answer to question three?" I asked, masochistically. "I put photosynthesis."

"It was phototropism, I think," said Susanna Forbes, butting in.

"Oh no! I'm going to fail!" I concluded, fully succumbing to postexam panic.

"It was worth eight marks, too," Susanna Forbes added gloomily.

"Well, at least you all filled something in. I left most of the paper blank." Bethan looked as if she might start to hyperventilate at any moment.

"Luke says these ones don't count anyway," said Poppy reassuringly once we were on the bus. French oral was the next day. Oh God Oh God Oh God.

"Just because *he* is doing his GCSEs," I said. "Ours still matter. Miss Rustford may have chilled out but she still keeps wincing at our French accents during our role-plays!"

"Holly, where is Miss Rustford from?"

"Milton Keynes."

"Exactly. What does she know?"

I figured out my timetable once I got home. Okay. I could cover one topic every fifteen minutes, which meant I could go to bed at one a.m. as long as I got up at five thirty a.m., which would give me two and a half hours to revise "Useful Phrases" and "Numbers."

Calm, I thought. Stay calm. Have some Jelly Babies.

Of Mice and Men

I T TOOK ABOUT TWENTY BILLION YEARS (okay, two weeks), but exams did finally finish and everyone I knew did actually survive! English was the very last exam, and it was actually okay. English is my best subject. Not that I said that to anyone else. I figured it wasn't the done thing when people were reassuring themselves that they would get marks for writing their name. French oral was *awful*, though. At the Zoo? We hadn't even done that one in the lesson. Also, how was I supposed to know that if you pronounce *"beaucoup"* wrong it sounded like *"beau cul,"* which means "beautiful arse"? I had a bad feeling about my French oral mark.

It felt fabulous when the exams were finally over. I didn't have to keep anything in my head anymore! Tra la laa. Then, on Friday before the youth club, Poppy invited me round to her house to celebrate being allowed out to see Jez again. As soon as I'd got into her room she took me by the shoulders and propelled me solemnly into the seat by her window. I giggled.

"Holly," she said seriously. "We have allowed ourselves to become distracted by exams. Exams, revision, and other boring things."

"Distracted from what?"

"From our New Year's resolutions, of course!"

"But—"

"Exams are over, we're allowed out again—let's do it!"

"Do what?"

"We had a list full of things to do, remember? The boys, the snogging . . . Jez, Luke . . ."

"What's brought this on?"

"I was reading this article." Poppy plucked a magazine from the pile beside her bed and handed it to me.

It said, *Make him yours!* with a picture of a smug-looking girl clinging on to a gorgeous male model.

"It says that boys are often useless at making a move and girls need to make things happen." Poppy grabbed the white halterneck top Claudia had given her and continued, muffled, as she pulled the top over her head.

"I haven't been seeing Jez enough, or moving things along. Now that exams are over I might just flirt a bit."

Blimey.

"So—what are you going to do about Luke?" Poppy continued as she went over to the mirror and covered herself with Impulse spray.

"I—what do you mean, what am I going to do about it?"

"Just what I said! You've got nothing to lose."

That was clearly not true. There is nearly always something to lose. I felt a bit panicky. "I could . . . I mean, I do want to make things happen and everything—but how can I?"

"Why not start a conversation?"

I laughed. "I'm not like you or Sasha."

Poppy looked for a moment as if she was going to say something, then didn't.

I looked down at the article. Her enthusiasm was endearing, but it was hopeless. While it was bound to happen for Poppy and Jez, and Claudia was sure to dazzle someone new before too long, how could I just engage Luke in conversation? What if I froze up or said something stupid?

I sighed. Poppy sighed as well and continued putting on makeup.

I carried on reading the article. Then, suddenly, a little cartoon-style lightbulb lit up in my head. "I know!"

"What?"

"I can write something down and read it out! It says so here!"

Poppy got up and peered over my shoulder. "No, it doesn't. It just says to talk about horoscopes."

"But—it's perfect! I could prepare one in advance!" I was thinking out loud now, fizzy with renewed hope. "I am good at writing things! I'll casually read Luke his horoscope from one of your magazines but secretly I'll write it in advance. He's not going to know I've written it down. Is he? And horoscopes are really open to interpretation, aren't they? It will be really subtle! But meaningful."

Poppy played with her mascara wand. "I know you can write down stuff for exams and things. But it doesn't really work like that with boys."

"But if I talked to him I might mess it up! With writing I can plan it in advance."

"But—"

"This," I said firmly, "is the perfect plan."

TO BE FAIR TO ME, THE PERFECT PLAN started off really well. When I went back round to Poppy's that Sunday, Luke was actually in Poppy's room, hunched in the chair by Mouse's cage! I shot Poppy a quizzical look.

"He's drawing Mouse while he's sleeping," Poppy explained as if Luke wasn't there. "He's doing art A-level next year."

"What, like . . . a still life?"

"I don't know. Let's go downstairs."

"Oh—but—you know—your parents are watching TV downstairs. We'll never be able to talk. We might as well stay up here."

Poppy rolled her eyes. "Oh yes. Well, in that case . . ." Poppy was just grumpy because after all that discussion and preparation the day before, Jez hadn't shown up at the youth club.

Delighted, I picked up an armful of magazines, deposited them on the bed next to me, and waited for a good moment. I was pleased with Luke's fake horoscope, having spent hours getting it right. (This is where school writing assignments have been going wrong. They simply needed a better incentive, such as the possibility of a snog with the love of your life at the end of them.)

Five minutes later Luke, pencil between teeth, muttered, "It's gone in the bloody toilet roll."

"He's a mouse," said Poppy. "Not an it. Animals do move, you know."

"Shut up!"

"You shut up!"

This was in danger of not developing according to plan. I made a meaningful face at Poppy and said, "Do you want to hear your horoscope, Poppy?"

"But it'll be out of da–," she began.

"It's still a good guide."

"Er—okay."

"Pisces," I read triumphantly from the real horoscopes, "is biding her time as always. With Mars on the ascendant, just be sure all is what it seems. Avoid big decisions around the time of the new moon."

Luke didn't seem to be listening at all, just frowning

and poking Mouse with his number two pencil. "It's moving too much."

"Well, you're poking him!"

Huh. Poppy didn't seem to be listening either.

Luke looked stormy. "I can't bloody draw it if—"

"So!" I butted in cheerily, to diffuse the situation. "Luke, what star sign are you?"

"What?"

"What star sign?" (I know! I know! Libra! But I am not going to say. How subtle is that!)

"I don't know."

"When is your birthday?"

"Sixth of October."

"Then you're Libra."

Poppy made a faint groaning sound, but I was determined. This was going to be a very subtle way of gently moving forward. It couldn't be bad. Honestly.

"Libra is perceptive," I began, reading from the folded bit of paper I'd tucked inside the horoscope pages, "but this time you don't realize what's right under your nose. Look closer to home and you'll find it's been worth waiting for this girl!"

Luke looked up. Hurrah.

"Don't you mean boy? Isn't that a girl's magazine?"

Drat. "Person, sorry, it says person."

"Right."

"Um . . . your moon is in Saturn while your sun house is ascending into Uranus," I improvised hastily to give all this an air of respectability.

"Don't, you'll hurt him!" Poppy suddenly shouted. It turned out this was aimed at Luke, who was attempting to take Mouse out of his cage.

"I won't," said Luke. "I've had an idea. I'm going to put it on the page and draw round it. It'll be much easier."

"Don't!" Poppy flung a magazine at Luke.

"Ooof!" Luke flicked sawdust from Mouse's cage into Poppy's hair. I paused, revising my opinion that girls with older brothers (automatic supply of older male acquaintances) had it made.

"Don't!" Poppy yelled.

"Don't!" mimicked Luke in a falsetto. "Try stopping me, Plop!"

"At least my name doesn't rhyme with puke!"

I leaped out of the way to avoid the ensuing tussle. Poppy's pile of magazines went flying, spreading across her bed in a messy ripple.

"What's this?" said Luke, pausing for breath while grasping Poppy's hair in one hand. A small rectangular card had slid from one of the magazines and landed by his elbow. I thought with horror for a moment that it was his specially written horoscope.

But it wasn't.

The Comedy of Errors

I HAD BEEN WONDERING IF THERE WAS ANY possibility that the situation was salvageable but when I told Sasha the following morning at school she bit her lip and said, "Oh God, Holly. First he didn't know who you were. Then he thought you were weird. Now he knows you're weird."

I groaned and put my head on the desk. I was going to have to kill Poppy. How could she have kept the postcard from the skiing trip? Why hadn't she DESTROYED IT? Oh God—the look on Luke's face as he looked up from the pink-inked message. Sort of surprise mixed with confusion. I know technically I had just said for Poppy to intercept it, not throw it away, but . . . for Cadbury's sake!

Poppy was being very rueful and apologetic. She

said she'd thought someone would see the postcard if she just put it in the bin. But she didn't have to put it in the bin at her house, did she? She could easily have gone into London in the dead of night and thrown it in the Thames, or shredded it and eaten it for security or . . . okay. I told myself not to overreact. After all, it would be fine as long as I didn't have to see Luke ever again.

I could practically hear Sasha's brain cogs whirring as she searched for something positive to say. "You could look at it like this," she managed just as the bell went. "You've given him a hint, if nothing else."

A *hint*? I gave him French kisses in pink ink. And, unless I had remembered wrongly, something about wanting him in my bedroom!

As if that was not enough boy drama for one week, something really odd happened in Friday's computing lesson. Well, two things. First, we got our results and Sasha got the same mark as me, which was unheard of! But more importantly, I got an e-mail from Stu! Slimy-Stu-the-Chest-Starer! I was supposed to be doing a project about spreadsheets but Miss Stevenson was on the other side of the room, so I checked my e-mails on the quiet (Mum reads over my shoulder if I log on at home). Stu's e-mail was dated the day before. It said:

Dear Holly,

I know we don't know each other very well but I really like you and would like to see you again. If you like me too, let me know and we can go out sometime.

Love Stu

Love? Eeek. I was torn between:

1. Wanting to kill Jez for having obviously given Stu my e-mail address.
2. Being marginally intrigued by getting an illicit message from a boy in a computing lesson (though, obviously, wishing it was from someone I actually fancied).
3. Being delighted to finally have someone that I would have to let down gently, like all deeply desirable people.

Stu was obviously just trying his luck, because otherwise he would have e-mailed me straight after the cinema, wouldn't he? There was no way I was going out with him. I was sure I could justify it without hurting his feelings. After all, I had a . . . er . . . busy life. That's it. A busy life with a list full of things to achieve this year. No time for a relationship!

Miss Stevenson announced that we had five minutes before lunch break, so I quickly typed a reply and hit SEND, just avoiding Miss Stevenson seeing it. As the bell went, I was about to shut down the computer when I saw a fresh e-mail in my inbox! I looked warily over at Miss Stevenson but she was on the other side of the room helping Rashida to print out her work. I covertly opened a second e-mail from Stu. Scary. Was he stalking me?

> Dear Holly,
>
> What can I say? It's lunch break so I just saw your message. Don't worry, I think it's really great when a girl knows what she wants. You're clearly a really special person. See you very soon, I hope.
>
> All yours, love Stu

Stu seemed to be handling the pain of my rejection by going into denial. Blimey. I'd basically told him to go away and he had come back for more. And he'd called me a special person! That was pretty flattering, to be honest. I would have asked Claudia for advice, but she was off ill with a toothache, so I had to remain confused. I covertly printed out Stu's e-mail thread along with my computing work and stuffed the e-mail quickly into my bag.

I was telling Poppy about Stu's unrequited love on the bus when Jez called me on my mobile!

"Do you want to speak to Poppy?" I asked.

"Well, actually I wanted to speak to you," said Jez. "I heard all about your e-mail to Stu—I was surprised, to be honest!"

I thought, Oh God, poor Stu. He must be really gutted if he's talking about it to Jez. Boys never discuss their feelings unless they're *really* upset.

"Oh, right," I said. I suddenly felt really bad. Did everyone think I should go out with him?

"No messing, straight to the point!"

I couldn't even find my voice to rebuke Jez for giving Stu my e-mail address. Jez didn't actually sound too bothered that I had rejected his friend, but I felt awful. I was a horrible, cruel person.

"Well, it's hard to say exactly what you mean via

e-mail," I said, waves of guilt washing over me. "I didn't really have time to go into detail. I didn't mean to—"

"No, no, it's fine!" interrupted Jez. "Don't worry! No further details required."

"You don't think I was too blunt?"

"No—I think he appreciated it. You might as well tell it like it is!"

God, I thought, Stuart must actually be quite sweet to think I am okay even though I have hurt his feelings! It was stressful being desired and waiting for exam results at the same time.

Poppy and I went round to her house so we could talk some more about Stu. Poppy ranted for five minutes because of a supply teacher who had read out the register wrong and called her Poopy. I think actually she was upset because Jez hadn't asked to speak to her.

"Jez probably didn't want to overdo it," I reassured her as we sat cross-legged on her bed, facing each other. "He's had exams too, remember. He did invite us round to his house, didn't he?"

Poppy looked unconvinced. She stared down at her duvet, biting the end of a pen.

"Call and say hi. He really likes you," I said

encouragingly. "We'll all go to the cinema again or something. Go on!"

"Ugh, I've got ink in my mouth."

"Don't change the subject!"

"What if I get ink poisoning?"

"Give me your mobile."

"No, I'll do it," Poppy claimed, but didn't appear to be moving, just looking sideways at the phone.

"Dial it!" I urged. I needed to go to the loo.

"You're full of confidence all of a sudden! What's brought this on?"

"Nothing."

"You're really flattered by Stu's e-mail, aren't you?"

"No."

Poppy raised an eyebrow.

"Well, yes, a bit," I conceded.

"Ooh, check you out!"

"Yes, well, no one's had an unrequited crush on me before!"

Poppy rolled her eyes. Honestly, I was just *saying*. I continued, "There's no way it's going to happen, but it's still massively flattering. He was so persistent, even when I put in my e-mail that I wasn't interested in having a relationship with him! It was like . . . you know, he's interested in my personality. Really, it's more flattering than physical attraction. It's quite cool, really; you think boys are really shallow and then they're not."

Poppy sighed deeply (clearly annoyed that I had a much better class of admirer than she did with Yves) and pressed the green button under Jez's number. I leaned forward in encouragement, only for Poppy to hold the phone out toward me. It was engaged.

ON THE WAY HOME FROM POPPY'S I saw Luke walking past. He looked sort of sweet and deadly sexy at the same time, but I crossed the road to avoid eye contact and subsequent embarrassment. Despite the confidence boost brought on by Stu's e-mails, I was just so mortified by Luke having read that postcard! Instead I dashed home, leaned out of my window, and stared after him in a wistful, Juliet-type way. Unfortunately Lorraine from Year Eleven was walking past the other way, lit up a cigarette, and looked up at me in apparent disdain. How rude!

I got changed out of my uniform and was on my way downstairs in an optimistic hunt for biscuits when I found Jamie and Evil Liam sniggering by my bags in the hall! Oh God, not my swimming cap again.

I sped over. "Get out of my bag! My swimming cap's not in there. And don't even think about changing my ringtone—hey!"

Evil Liam was holding up the printout of Stu's e-mail!

I tried to grab it. "That's mine! Mum!"

"D'you really want her to see this?" said Evil Liam, who I clearly should have named Very Evil Liam. I glared at him and looked down at the printout.

That was when I noticed two things. First, my original reply to Stu had printed out as part of the e-mail thread. Second, my reply actually read as follows:

> Hi Stud,
> I'm not really looking for a relationship—I am very busty at the moment and need to do lustful things . . . I hope that is okay.
>
> From Holy

What?

"I am very busty!" repeated Evil Liam, laughing as if he was going to collapse.

I just stared at the page, an inarticulate squeaking noise coming from the back of my throat.

"What?" I finally murmured. "Stu. Not . . . Stud. I need to do a *list full of things* . . . not lustful things . . . oh God." How could this have happened?

I stuffed the message into my jeans pocket, glaring at Evil Liam.

Hi Stud.

Very busty.

Oh God.

T CAME TO ME LATE ON FRIDAY NIGHT AND I called Sasha immediately on my mobile.

"It's midnight!" she complained groggily. "And you sound muffled."

"I'm in my wardrobe so I don't wake up my mum. But that's not the point. Listen—did you cheat in the computing exam?"

"What?"

"Did you cheat?"

"Well, er . . . I still had to type the stupid bit of text. But yes, I turned on the auto-spell checker. It's brilliant! Does the words as you go along, so no one sees. I did your machine, as well, while I was at it."

I took a deep breath and accidentally inhaled a feather from the feather boa in my wardrobe. Spluttering slightly, I said, "You do realize that it sometimes changes words you don't want to change?"

"So? We both still got eighty-six percent, didn't we? That's pretty good."

Aaarggh!

I WENT SHOPPING WITH POPPY ON SATURDAY, officially to erase postcard trauma from my mind and unofficially to erase e-mail trauma, as well. I hadn't brought myself to mention the incident to Poppy yet. How could I tell her? It was just too raw and humiliating, after having been so flattered by Stu's persistence! Urgh. I couldn't even bring myself to tell Sasha what she'd done.

It was just plain embarrassing that Stu and presumably all his friends now thought I was a raving nymphomaniac. Despite recklessly spending my pocket money on some Body Shop conditioner, I couldn't get the e-mail out of my mind, not helped by the fact that the stupid e-mail printout was still in my jeans pocket where I'd left it. I couldn't exactly chuck it out because Poppy would see! I could imagine the conversation. "What's that?" "Oh, Stu thought I wanted to leap on him." "Oh my God, and you thought he was really brokenhearted!" (followed by hysterical giggling).

In McDonald's, I couldn't even choose what to eat because I was so distracted. I decided I would ask Jez in utter secrecy to set Stu straight. (Mercifully he hadn't phoned Poppy to tell her about it.) I could ask him to keep it to himself, then I could file the incident into the bit of my mind marked *Never Think about This Again!*

Poppy and I were leaving McDonald's with our takeaway meals when we saw a familiar silhouette in one of the queues.

"Claudia!" called out Poppy. Claudia turned around in a swoosh of dark hair, eyebrows raised in surprise, and edged her way out of the queue. "Hello!" she said brightly. "Are you shopping, then?"

"I just got this jacket," began Poppy as she pulled it from its bag. "We went to a billion shops and in the end I went back and got the first one I saw!"

"Great!" said Claudia. She was playing nervously with her embroidered purse and abruptly stopped when she saw me looking. "Well, nice to see you!" she said swiftly. "Better go. You don't want your food to get cold."

She walked back toward the queue and we turned to leave. I was just registering that Claudia was being a bit weird—sounding like somebody's mum, for starters—when Poppy stopped dead in her tracks.

"There's Jez!"

There was Jez. He was alone at a table, leaning back in his bolted-down chair. For a moment he was looking right in our direction without seeing us. Then, his eyes focused on us standing there like idiots, clutching our brown paper bags.

He wasn't in there alone; he was waiting for someone.

Claudia.

Paradise Lost

Y OU COULD HAVE HEARD A FRENCH FRY drop. Silently, Poppy looked over at where Claudia was queuing, then back at Jez. I saw Claudia turn fleetingly and I caught her eye for a split second. Panicked, she turned away.

Jez half rose to his feet. "Hello!" he called out with a kind of strangled breeziness. "God, what a surpr—"

Poppy didn't wait for the full sentence. She accelerated out of the restaurant, almost going flying over a yellow cone marking a wet bit of floor. She didn't stop until she got to the park. I ran after her and sat down next to her, catching my breath. Breathing raggedly, Poppy got her burger and fries out of their brown paper bag and sat them on her lap. I didn't know what to say.

"He can do what he wants," Poppy managed finally

in a tiny voice. "It's not as if we were going out together, is it?"

I put my hand on Poppy's shoulder as she ripped at a ketchup sachet with her fingernails. It wouldn't open. "Stupid thing!" she exclaimed. And that's when she burst into tears.

W E DECIDED THAT SHOPPING WAS NO longer a top priority and went home—Poppy wanted to be by herself for a bit. As we said good-bye, she paused.

"Holly . . . could you find out what's been going on? See if everyone knows except me?"

I nodded. "Of course."

I sat in my hall by the phone, trying to take it all in. Drat. Suddenly it was a really bad time to be out of phone credit. Fortunately Dad was in the shed mending Jamie's Rollerblades, so I could avoid his monologues about talking-on-the-phone-when-your-friends-live-so-close-by. Mum was in the garden, which was a bit more risky, but hopefully she would stay there.

I thought about calling Jo, but then stopped mid-dial. After all, she was friends with Claudia—what could I say? So I hung up and called Sasha, who was really sweet. She was obviously shocked but just asked if Poppy was okay without even saying "I told you so," even though she had been right about Claudia all along. Clearly Sasha and Claudia were not that similar, after all, as Sasha had some integrity. Sasha phoned Bethan (Gossip Central) for the lowdown, then called me back. I was practically camped out next to the phone. It was like Emergency Headquarters in my hall. Unfortunately, Poppy called back before I'd figured out how best to tell her the news.

"What have you found out?" said Poppy, sniffling. She sounded muffled, as if she was under her duvet.

"Um," I said hesitantly, looking at a shadow. I knew it! Mum had come in and had suddenly decided to hover nearby. She was pretending to water the plants.

"Tell me!"

"It's just . . . well . . . I called Sasha who spoke to Bethan and . . . apparently Claudia and Jez bunked off school on Friday to go up to London."

Silence. I swallowed and continued in lowered tones, "Bethan heard Claudia talking to Tanya about it in the locker room. She didn't realize Claudia was talking about Jez until now."

Understandably, Poppy's voice turned a little high-pitched. "Bunked off?"

"I know." I winced.

"That was *our thing*! That's what he said to me! Like in *Ferris Bueller's Day Off*!"

"I know."

"So . . . she wasn't at home with a toothache, watching her stupid mother on daytime TV?"

"No. She wrote the sick note herself. They went shopping in Selfridges for her holiday stuff."

"He KNEW he'd said that to me!"

Mum was still around, now apparently straightening the shoes in the hall cupboard. I lowered my voice even further. "I know. It's really out of order."

"How could they?"

"They've got no morals. They deserve each other."

Poppy's voice went very quiet and wobbly. "I know I said I wanted to be alone, but would you come round? Only if you don't mind."

I took a deep breath. I really didn't want to risk bumping into Luke ever again after the postcard humiliation, but this was important! "Of course. I'll be five minutes."

I persuaded Dad to give me next week's pocket

money early—I must have looked totally desperate—and ran to the newsagent's, a burst of energy reserved for emergencies only. I sped into Poppy's room clutching a magazine I had bought for her, only to find Luke sitting next to Poppy on the bed! Oh God. I really didn't want to see him. Luke had picked up a tan on study leave and looked, irritatingly, even more gorgeous than usual. His hair had slight blond highlights in it from the sun and his green eyes were standing out. (As in, emphasised by tan. Not popping out, cartoon-style.) I was stuck between the desire to run straight back out of the house and my usual wish to fling myself at him. I managed to sit down on the other side of Poppy and held tightly on to the bed, releasing one hand only to give Poppy the magazine, which had a free sample of Hide the Red tinted foundation (free samples have magical cheering-up properties).

Poppy said thank you then promptly burst into tears. Looking a little alarmed, Luke put his arm around Poppy and patted her awkwardly on the back. We were within about a centimeter of touching each other. Except it was actually a much wider gap than that, metaphorically speaking, because he thought I was a complete idiot.

Luke being nice had the effect of making Poppy cry some more. She stuttered, "He went into-into-

London with HER, I mean, FINE—and now I'm—all—by—myself—and—"

"It's okay," I said soothingly. I appealed with my eyes for Luke to say something supportive, but he didn't appear to have a clue how to deal with the situation. In fact, he appeared totally lost! I never knew that about him before—he'd always seemed so cool. For a moment he seemed as lost around girls and their emotions as I was around boys.

"You're not all by yourself, you've got loads of friends!" I ventured. I looked at Luke again, who shrugged helplessly.

"I know what you need," I told Poppy, "Some chocolate. I'll be back in a second."

Luke looked a bit panicked. "I'll come with you!"
Blimey.

I went downstairs, followed by Luke saying, "I'll help. I know where everything is." He tried to overtake as we reached the kitchen door but we misjudged and bumped right into each other. I held on to the doorframe. "After you," I managed.

Luke walked over and reached up to the top cupboards, rummaged for a bit, and produced a tin of hot chocolate. "Will this do?"

"This is an emergency. Does your Mum have any of the real stuff?"

We looked at each other, then set about quickly opening the cupboards and looking for Dairy Milk, Twixes, anything. He looked at the high cupboards. I took the low ones and eventually I found a multipack of Double Deckers. "Bingo!" I said, bouncing upright and bumping right into Luke again. Not just knee-bumping. A full-on body bump. "Sorry," we both said simultaneously. I held on tightly to the worktop and tried to subdue a ripple of lust. Forget about it, Holly.

He looked at me. I felt as if the air was crackling with tension. Or maybe it was just the sound of the multipack wrapper.

"Better take these upstairs," I said, and ran up the stairs, in case my resolve weakened.

Poppy was in exactly the same place on her bed, sniffing gently to herself. When I handed her a Double Decker she smiled wanly and put it down, untouched.

This was really serious.

Luke and I sat back down on either side of Poppy.

"You know what?" I attempted, since we were clearly back to square one. "You don't need Jez. We'll have a great summer being young, free, and single."

Poppy's face crumpled. "We're—not even—*going* anywhere. And you've got Stu after you! Even if you don't like him—he really likes you! He's . . . obsessed!"

Hmm. Pulling the printed e-mail from my jeans pocket and regaling the whole stupid saga would really cheer Poppy up. But there was no way I could do that—Luke was there! It was too humiliating. What could I say, exactly? "Oh, it turns out that instead of being deeply in love with me, Stu just thinks I am a nymphomaniac." No, Luke would just think I was the most pathetic person in the universe.

"You'll probably"—Poppy gasped for breath—"double date with Jez and Claudia!"

How ironic that Poppy was now paranoid about me leaving *her* out. But it was even more sad that she believed Stu really liked me, when actually I had got it all wrong.

"No, I won't," I said, sighing.

"You might do! You'll go off with her!"

I looked at Poppy, red-faced and woeful, then sneaked a look at Luke, all gorgeous and concerned. I thought, I could tell her. It would cheer her up. But how could I make a fool of myself in front of Luke? Again? When I really fancied him? But then I thought,

oh sod it. Cheering Poppy up was of primary impor-
tance now. And Luke already thought I was a total idiot.

"No, I won't. Really. Look at this."

At first Poppy looked uncomprehendingly as I
pulled the e-mail printout from my jeans pocket and
gave it to her. "What's this?"

"Stu isn't obsessed with me," I explained. "Well, he
certainly isn't in love. He misunderstood."

"What?"

"The spell checker was on, but I didn't realize. Like
here, I meant to write 'busy,' but it ended up as 'busty.'
And, um, I meant to write 'list full,' but I must have left
out the space because it got changed to 'lustful.' He got
the impression I was, er . . . after his body."

Poppy squinted, red-eyed, at the printout. "Oh my
God. How totally embarrassing."

"I know."

"And you thought—"

"I know."

"Are you okay?"

"I'm all right," I said. "At least I didn't thank him
for his massage. Or suggest meeting in a pubic place."

Poppy sniffed a bit and looked at the e-mail again.
Then, thank God, she started giggling. It was a bit weak

at first, but then got stronger, until it was full-on laughter. I glanced quickly at Luke, saw that, sure enough, he was laughing too. I looked away.

"I'm going to go now," I said weakly, standing up.

I know I had wanted Poppy to cheer up, but suddenly I'd had enough of being laughable. How could I just sit in the same room as Luke after this, and the postcard and the hundred small stupid things I'd done or said around him? Poppy had lost Jez and meanwhile I looked like a complete idiot. An idiot with no holiday, no Luke—no nothing.

The Age of Reason

I WENT BACK HOME AND CALLED SASHA, THEN remembered she was probably out seeing Darren. So I sat in the hall trying hard not to cry, when Mum came back AGAIN, this time pretending to tidy up takeaway menus.

"Don't worry, whatever it is," she said blithely. "You always did take things to heart!"

I didn't respond. Undeterred, Mum wandered into the kitchen but unfortunately remained audible.

"I remember how upset you were when you were little and tried to make perfume with that jar of rose petals and water in the cupboard. Went moldy after a week, of course! Now stay off the phone and put your shoes on. Jamie's got the final of his football tournament."

I really, really didn't feel like it. I sighed and located my shoes that Mum had tidied to the back of the hall cupboard, wishing that she would let me stay in by myself. If only I was Mouse, I wouldn't have to worry about any of this.

I took my rough book along in the car and sat shivering at the edge of the football pitch, trying to ignore the sudden clouds while I wrote a list:

LATEST SUMMARY OF MY LIFE

1. Luke knows I am an idiot.
2. I said "beautiful arse" to Miss Rustford in my French oral.
3. Jez has abandoned Poppy for Claudia.
4. I have failed tons of resolutions. My bottom is no smaller than in January, and Poppy and I have failed to get to go on holiday sans parents.
5. I was a stupid child who tried to make perfume out of rose petals.
6. I just wished I was a mouse.

Then I decided, masochistically, to update my Who-Likes-Who chart:

WHO-LIKES-WHO CHART, VERSION TWO

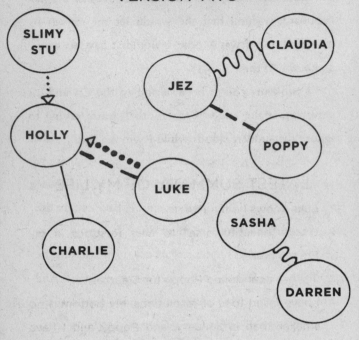

KEY

Broken line: Zero hope.

Wiggly line: Going out with and is

sublimely happy, pah.

Thin line: Snogged once and it was rubbish

so what was the point?

Thin dotted arrow: Thinks is nympho.

Thick dotted arrow: Thinks is idiot.

 198

Suddenly it started to rain, covering the Who-Likes-Who chart with wet splotches. I had just closed the book when a player kicked the football too wide and slammed it right into my chest!

"Sorry!" called someone.

"You okay, Holly?" shouted Jamie from the pitch.

Ouch. That really hurt! I half waved to indicate I was okay and turned to Mum, bent double.

"Are you okay?" she asked, and put her hand on my shoulder. But I caught a hint of frustration in her voice, and I knew she felt her daughter should have caught the ball, or perhaps been made of iron. I looked away quickly so as not to suddenly start crying, not about the stupid football, but about her. And Poppy and Jez. And Luke. I put my rough book on my head to shield my hair from the rain and stared bleakly at the pitch.

SCHOOL HAD BECOME REALLY SCARY AND tense. Poppy and Claudia were in an icy stand-off and Not Speaking. It was really awkward. Everyone had heard what had happened, but no one wanted to bring it up. And it meant I had to keep out of Jo's way too! I just didn't know what to say to her, seeing as she was friends with Claudia. I didn't think I could just act neutrally about it. Meanwhile, I was getting Poppy to leave earlier in the mornings so I didn't have to see Luke on the bus!

In a bizarre reminder of life before it all went wrong, more exam results started coming through. I got eighty-seven percent in English! Then one night I correctly answered a question about chocolate while Dad was watching *University Challenge*! All this triggered a small but significant shift in my world outlook. As there was clearly no romantic or holiday-type happiness for me in this life, I made a decision. I would be an Academic Goddess instead and be completely absorbed in work. Nothing would be able to hurt me, *as I was not like normal people.*

The next day, I did some optional background reading for history! I would take the opportunity to learn more about the Russian Revolution. I would probably take my GCSEs early, as a profitable use of all the time I would save not caring about boys or how I looked. I even went to the library and got out *Les liaisons dangereuses* in French to read on the bus.

Poppy came over to my house that night, because she didn't want to be alone and I didn't want to see

Luke. There was only just space for us both in my room, what with all my school books and extra reading.

"Can't we go up to Ivy's room?" said Poppy.

"Mum won't let us."

"You should swap. She's hardly here anymore."

I sighed, got up, and checked there was no one listening at the door, "Mum wouldn't take it too well. I'd rather just not go into it. Anyway, how are you feeling?"

"Awful," said Poppy.

Hmm. I had always wanted life to be more eventful and like a film, but I had imagined going to cool beach parties and riding around in convertibles, not big, bad dramatic events where people got hurt.

"I tell you what, we are NEVER going to the youth club again," muttered Poppy.

"Whatever you think is best," I said. I was totally not bothered about the end of knee-bumping for me and Luke. Definitely. Not. At. All.

"Well, at least you snogged Charlie," said Poppy.

"That was crap."

"Was it?"

"Yup."

"Er—Holly—are you okay? You seem different."

I told Poppy about my new Academic Goddess plan.

She sounded concerned that I was giving up boys and seemed to think I wouldn't have anything to occupy my mind! I told her this was ridiculous, considering all the intellectual stuff that I would be focusing on.

"Boys are far too much trouble," I concluded. There was a silence. I added, "Anyway, listen, are you okay about Jez?"

Jez had called me on the way home to ask "how Poppy was doing." I had been as frosty as I could manage for such a hot day. (I had clearly been nominated the neutral one, but I wasn't really sure how to act in this situation—pretend Poppy was fine, or tell Jez she was so depressed she couldn't even listen to the radio because it was all love songs?) I had held out the phone to Poppy, but she shook her head vehemently and mouthed, "Find out." So I eventually got it out of Jez that he and Claudia snogged when her cab was late that time at Jez's house. It had started when Jez had to comfort Claudia because she was "really worried about the cab being late." God, boys are like oblivious, bumbling creatures sometimes, plodding along while the girls plot and scheme around them. Then again I was so busy being grown-up and not hating Claudia that I somehow missed her scheme too! Whilst on the phone to Jez, I eventually told him about the e-mail to Stu. Jez laughed rather too much, if you ask me, but he did say he'd set the record straight.

"I feel so stupid," began Poppy through a mouthful of chocolate. She swallowed and started again. "I thought *something* funny was going on at Jez's. You know, Claudia trying on his football shirt and all that, but I thought I was being paranoid!"

Hmm. Pure, unadulterated flirting. All of it. Typical of someone who was constantly checking her reflection in shop windows.

"I didn't think—I thought Claudia wouldn't—I'm never speaking to her again!" Poppy burst out tearfully.

"Have you spoken to her yet, at all?"

Poppy shook her head. "Nope. She's avoiding me, isn't she? When stuff gets difficult, she disappears."

Half a bar of chocolate and several girl power tunes later we were going through a long list of stuff Poppy should have said to Jez in McDonald's that, sadly, we had only thought of today.

"What about 'Go to hell, both of you. I hope you choke on your Chicken McNuggets'?"

"Or, 'I'd throw my Regular Fanta over you right now, except I'm thirsty and *you're not worth it.*'"

Poppy giggled, then changed the subject. "I can't believe your e-mail to Stu!"

I was so pleased it was still a source of amusement.

"You'd think he would have realized it was just my dodgy typing," I said ruefully. "Anyway, I can spell, I was just writing too fast, that's all. 'Busy' I wrote. 'BUSY.'"

"After that postcard I would have thought you'd have given up writing to boys," said Poppy.

"Well, I've given up boys now. For good! And, I *did* say I wasn't looking for a relationship. It was OBVIOUS."

"I think Stu thought that meant your were up for some . . . some no-strings fun!" said Poppy, giggling. She paused, looked at me, and whispered, "I am very busty," in a mock-sultry voice, as if it was hysterically funny.

"Horrible, sex-obsessed boys!" I ranted.

Poppy broke off a whole row of chocolate, stacked the pieces one on top of the other, then stuck them all in her mouth at once. There was a silence where she chewed. I gnawed at another piece, grating it into my mouth with my teeth.

It was weird. I guess I had Poppy to myself again

now, but somewhere in the back of my mind I still really wanted to talk to Poppy about having gone off with Claudia at the start of the year. I mean, Claudia had sealed her own fate, but it hardly settled the friendship issue—it wasn't as if the Wicked Witch of the West was dead and I could dance about like a munchkin in *The Wizard of Oz*. Okay, I had accidentally tumbled into first place, friendship-wise, but did it mean much, or was I the only remaining option? Don't get me wrong, I didn't need declarations of lifelong friendship or blood rituals or anything, I just wanted to feel comfortable; that if I shared a secret it wouldn't be used against me later on; that friendship wasn't instantly dissolved when someone more cool turned up. I finished my bit of chocolate and debated it all in my head. Bringing my thoughts into the open would stop me pondering them in the back of my mind for ever more. But what did it matter that I felt secure when Poppy was this upset about Jez? It would just sound like I was saying "I told you so"! Now was not the time.

So I just offered her some more chocolate.

War and Peace

I SHOULD HAVE GUESSED THAT POPPY AND Claudia would have a showdown at some point, I just didn't know it would be during French. In the last ten minutes of Wednesday's lesson, Miss Rustford split us into our usual groups for French oral practice. Nightmare! We congregated reluctantly around a spare desk, in a distinctly awkward silence. I exchanged looks with Sasha from across the room who mouthed, "Good luck!"

Poppy thudded down into a chair, cleared her throat, and pointedly put down her textbook. Claudia remained standing, wrapping a bit of sleek, dark hair round one finger.

I looked at them both. "So . . . ," I said valiantly. "Page thirty, prepositions."

Poppy sighed and pushed her textbook away. "I'm not in the mood," she said, glaring at the desk.

Claudia looked a bit scared and started zipping and unzipping her Kookaï pencil case. "I didn't mean for you to just bump into us like that," she finally ventured.

"So, when did you plan on telling me the truth?" Poppy said, clearly unable to contain herself any longer.

"Sur la table et sous la chaise," Claudia responded (not entirely satisfactorily) as Miss Rustford paused beside our desk in a leisurely circuit of the classroom.

"Au dessous de la fenêtre," I added for good measure.

"We just . . . get on well," Claudia hissed as Miss Rustford moved on in her mission to make as many groups as possible feel paranoid about their French accents. "He said he couldn't help being attracted to me."

Hmm. Using the "I'm just more attractive than you" argument wasn't the best plan for reestablishing a friendship. Poppy made an indiscriminate "Hmmph" noise (quite French-sounding actually, although I think it was unintentional). Annoyingly, I could imagine that Jez and Claudia looked really good together. He was all blond and English-looking, Claudia was all dusky and Mediterranean—like walking illustrations captioned *Opposites Attract*. Then again, they were both image-conscious, glossy, and rich, so maybe they were quite similar.

"Come on," said Claudia in a let's-lay-our-cards-on-the-table tone of voice. "It's not as if you were going out. You hadn't even kissed."

Bad move.

"Huh!" said Poppy in a pinched voice. "It's funny how sometimes things—like friends—get in the way!"

"Poppy!" said Miss Rustford, evidently failing to spot any French at all in this sentence, let alone a preposition. On cue, the bell went for afternoon break. Everyone else leaped to their feet and started talking. Poppy sniffed contemptuously and gathered her stuff together, pointedly looking away.

"I'm sorry," Claudia said, trying a new, probably unfamiliar, tactic.

"Let's go, Poppy," I said bravely, in my new role as professional side-taker.

Then, suddenly it was all about me.

"Oh, for God's sake," snapped Claudia. "At least the boys I fancy don't think I'm a freak who sends postcards full of complete rubbish."

I stared at Claudia and it dawned on me that all the bad feelings inside us never actually went away. They'd only been buried. I started to back off but then, suddenly, something hit me. I felt as if all my life I had been nothing but an agreeable shell, while inside was a mass of difficult questions I'd never asked, and argumentative things I'd never said. Come and watch badminton again, Holly! Have the smallest room, Holly! Let me ignore you for ages, Holly, you'll still be my friend when I'm done!

Why should I put up with all this? I'd had enough of it all, especially of Claudia, who clearly had a makeup bag where her heart should be. Poppy opened her mouth, but I got in there first.

"I don't care what you say about me," I told Claudia.

Claudia smirked and opened her mouth, but I wasn't finished. Shivery and suddenly full of adrenaline, I continued. "But I do care if you're going out with Jez. Because he really liked Poppy. I'm sure he did! And you got in the way."

There was a brief but satisfying pause. Claudia looked shell-shocked. Poppy looked taken aback too for a moment, but then added, "Exactly. And Luke never liked you, did he? So you can't talk." She gave Claudia a satisfyingly icy stare, picked up both our

French books, and walked off! I followed her.

Poppy sat down on a bench in the playground and pulled me into the spot next to her.

"You were really good!" she said, as if I deserved a My First Argument reward badge.

"I'd just had enough," I said. "Of Claudia. Of everything."

What I meant was, "Like when you went off with Claudia earlier in the year." It appeared you didn't need a degree in rocket science to figure this out, because Poppy looked down and finally said openly, "That wasn't ideal, was it?"

Normally I would have said, "Oh no, it's fine, don't worry!" then changed the subject. But my run-in with Claudia had, somehow, given me some oomph. It felt good to have at last said what I thought. Certainly, by not having arguments, I avoided disturbing the peace and guaranteed that I would have friends. But then, the only person who ever got hurt was myself! And maybe if I never said what I felt, I would be surrounded by friends but still feel alone.

So I looked straight at Poppy and said, "I felt really betrayed when you went off with Claudia. It was really horrible."

Poppy looked pained. But she didn't leap up and yell, "Criticism? The friendship is over!"

I continued, "I don't want to make you feel bad, but since you asked . . ."

"It got a bit mean," interrupted Poppy. "It wasn't supposed to. But—you kind of get caught up in her little world for a while too. You know?"

I nodded. I did know, after all.

"And later, with the matchmaking," Poppy continued, "I wanted someone who could sort that out for me. She was so impressive with boys." She laughed ruefully. "Too impressive."

"It was fine more recently, though," I said. "You know, when we were all planning stuff together. But— I felt as if you might just go off again any time you liked. And the Luke thing at the start of the year—that was horrid. You left me out of stuff and let her go on about fancying Luke in front of me. You knew that would make me feel really bad and you still did it."

Poppy looked really miserable. "Sorry. I was just annoyed about that text you sent Sasha. And Claudia was a new friend to me, and had so much . . . freedom and stuff. I shouldn't have used the Luke thing. I know it was really mean."

Poppy had tears in her eyes. I didn't want to make her feel worse. I felt the old, nonconfrontational Holly come hurtling back into my brain waving big signs saying, "Make it better! Don't complain!"

"Look . . . ," I said, struggling a bit. "It doesn't matter anymore. It's not going to happen with Luke anyway."

"No!" said Poppy vehemently. "It is important. Yes, Claudia liked Luke. But this is more about us. I didn't mean for it to be something that we—you know— used to make you feel bad. It just sort of happened." There was a pause, then Poppy added, "I mean, you and I have known each other for ages and stuff. I can talk to you about anything! And I feel a bit stupid now."

"Why?"

"It's pretty obvious, isn't it? That Claudia only wanted to be friends with me because of Luke. As soon as he wasn't interested she was off like a shot." Poppy added bitterly, "Until she spotted Jez, that is. Then she was back."

The Luke thing sounded about right. But Jez, too? It was just so strange, when Claudia could have anyone she wanted. What was she, some sort of archvillainess out to ruin her friends' lives?

"I was so sure you were going to get a happy ending," I said finally. "You know, like in films and stuff."

"And—that book."

"*Anne of Green Gables*. I'm really sorry it didn't happen."

Poppy hugged me. "It's okay."

WE WENT ROUND TO POPPY'S AFTER school to sit in her garden, since Luke was still out. I took my books so I could be an Academic Goddess and talk, as well. We settled ourselves on sun loungers, Poppy with her mobile in front of her in case Jez called to plead for forgiveness.

"It's so hot!" Poppy complained. We were both still in school uniform. "I'm getting changed."

She came back in shorts and a T-shirt, clutching her white halterneck. "Here, put this on. In fact, keep it."

"Are you sure?"

"It will really suit you. I want you to have it."

I went inside and got changed and admired myself in Poppy's bedroom mirror. It really was a lovely top.

Then I went back outside and lay on my sun lounger and told Poppy all the right things. You know, Claudia is really ugly, I hope she fails all her exams and that Arsenal never wins another game. But I don't think it helped much.

After a few minutes of peace, Mum rang on my mobile.

"Where are you?"

"I'm doing my homework round at Poppy's."

There was a silence, meaning she had other plans for me. "Holly, you'd better head back now. We're all going to badminton."

I could just imagine her in the hall, in one of her pastel tracksuits, ready to subject me to another evening of sportiness.

"Can I just stay here at Poppy's instead?"

Mum said smoothly, "No—you'll get back to the house before us."

"Is that really a problem?"

"Holly! You know you're not old enough to be in the house by yourself."

I took a deep breath. "Why don't I just wait at Poppy's until you're back?"

"Holly—you're coming along with us. It'll be fun.

Come home and put your trainers on. It's a nice day."

I glanced at Poppy, who was lying, oblivious, with her eyes closed. I took a deep breath.

"Mum, I know you think it's fun, but I don't."

I can only imagine that for once Mum's hearing failed her, because there was a short pause and then she said, "Pardon?"

"I'm not going to come this time," I said. "You're right—it's a lovely day. I want to stay here and enjoy it with Poppy in her garden. I'll talk to you later."

With that, I put down the phone and stared at it. The next time we spoke I would explain a bit more nicely that I had tried really hard to humor her and not let her down, but that I just wasn't like the rest of them. She was going to have to accept it! And maybe I should ask to move into Ivy's old room, after all. I sat there, feeling that it had been a bit of a mammoth day, when Poppy opened one eye and squinted at me.

"You okay?"

"Fine," I said.

"My mum bought ice lollies," said Poppy. "Do you want one?"

"Um—that would be lovely," I said.

I closed my eyes. I heard the creak of the sun

lounger as Poppy got up, and then there was quiet, apart from the distant sound of Mouse going round in his wheel. It was really nice feeling the sun on my face. I felt much better with life in general now I'd worked things out with Poppy—and got out of badminton! But I still hated that Poppy was so unhappy about Jez. The only thing I could think of that might actually cheer her up was getting to go on holiday, but Mum was hardly likely to say yes. My chances were even slimmer now I'd become a Bad Daughter.

"I've done that as well," said Luke's voice, suddenly.

Eeek! I tried to sit up and look dignified. It was difficult because after lying in the sun with my eyes closed my vision had gone funny and everything was blue-tinted.

"What—told Poppy you'd have an ice lolly?" I said confusedly.

"Fallen victim to so-called helpful spell checkers. Like your e-mail. But with text messages mostly."

Luke (blue and hazy but still irritatingly gorgeous) walked over and sat down on Poppy's vacated sun lounger.

At the start of the year I would have waited in stricken silence for Poppy to get back. But that was back when I thought if I wanted Luke enough I would get him. When actually, life wasn't like that. And I'd given up boys. So I said to myself: Holly, there are more important things in your life than whether you're saying the right things to Luke. Just say whatever comes into your head! Just pretend he's a girl or something.

Luke sipped from a carton of juice he was holding in one hand, and got out his mobile with the other. The phone was the shiny silver kind with a camera in it.

"With phones, it's predictive text that's the problem," said Luke. "Say you're trying to meet up with people in a bar." He flipped open the phone with one hand so I could see the screen, typed *bar* and *car* came up first.

"So people are always trying to find you in a car when you're in a bar?" It was quite surprising that Luke made daft mistakes too. Maybe he actually was just like a girl. You know, underneath the apparent boyness.

"Well, theoretically. I can't actually get into bars."

"Does it happen with other words?"

"I don't know," said Luke. He typed in *Poppy*. It came up *Sorry*, which was quite amusing.

"My phone doesn't even have predictive text. But

we did do anagrams of our names a while ago," I said. "Poppy's was 'ply party poo.'"

"Ha! What would mine be?"

I squinted at him and paused before answering. "God . . . um, 'lola turkey'?"

He squinted in concentration as he checked this out.

"That's impressive! You're quite clever, you know."

This was immensely gratifying. I didn't mention that "Luke Taylor" had been the first one I'd worked out, ages ago.

Luke laughed. "What was yours?"

"I only found a really rubbish one, erm . . . 'wholly lest lock.'"

"Sounds like Shakespeare or something."

"D'you think?"

"Definitely. *Hamlet* maybe. We watched the film as part of English GCSE."

"The one with Kate Winslet as Ophelia? I've seen that too."

There was a silence. I noticed, surprisingly, that it was a comfortable one.

"So your phone doesn't have predictive text?" asked Luke.

"No."

"Show me," said Luke curiously.

Hmm. I once ran a marathon rather than show Luke my knackered old phone (during What Would You Rather, obviously, not in real life).

I showed him. He tried not to laugh. "That's ancient!"

"I know," I said.

"But I am sure there are worse ones. Like in those old films from the eighties. You know, where all the mobile phones are huge bricks."

"Oh God, yes—I know what you mean. I think there might have been one in *Cocktail*. Not sure. Something with Tom Cruise in it, anyway."

"I've seen that film," said Luke. "I wanted to run off to Jamaica and be a barman for about a month afterward."

"And I wanted to be a beautiful, penniless artist who was actually really rich!"

We both looked up as Poppy wandered back into the garden clutching a selection of frozen snacks.

"Holly—she bought choc ices as well! Do you—"

It was quite amusing. Poppy stopped mid-sentence when she saw me talking to Luke, then managed, "Puke! That's my seat. Get out."

Luke got up, took an ice lolly from Poppy, said, "Ladies, I will take my leave," and did a sort of mock bow before going back into the house.

Poppy looked at him, then at me. "Er—what was that?"

"Nothing," I said.

She sat down and looked at me. "Why are you holding on to the sun lounger so tightly?"

"No reason." I looked back toward the house, a reflex from Mum always being in earshot, and said, "But, it's odd, though. He was talking to me. Normally!"

"Well, were you talking normally to him?" said Poppy, with a trace of "Duh!" in her voice.

"Yes, but that's because I've given up boys. What's the point trying to make it happen when I always make such an idiot of myself?" Poppy sighed for some reason, so I gave an example. "Like with that stupid e-mail story! Luke heard that. How embarrassing!"

"But, Holly, you know he just thought the e-mail story was funny?"

"Well, he was laughing at me. Like you were."

"Well, it *was* funny," said Poppy, "but he wasn't laughing *at* you, as in he thought you were really stupid.

It was just an amusing story, so he laughed. He was laughing to himself for ages after you left."

"But I don't want him to think I'm funny. I want him to fancy me."

"And how do you think that happens? You talk normally—you know, get on. Make a connection. Have conversations. I don't think you'd ever said anything much around him—at all—before that story!"

I looked at my ice lolly, which was melting at the bottom. "It's difficult to talk to boys."

"They're not a different species, you know."

"It's easy for you. I don't know how you do it." I licked the base of the lolly.

"You just did it! There's no magic formula, you know. You laugh, you chat, the boy talks back. You know, almost as if he's a normal human being." I swallowed a big bite of lolly too quickly, which gave me one of those painful cold headaches.

Poppy sighed. "Holly, don't take offense, but you only have trouble when you build it up into a huge big deal and worry far too much about boys liking you. You're okay with Jez, aren't you? You know why—it's because you don't fancy him. So you can see him for what he is—another normal human being. You don't have to write stuff down, or worry about how to act. And it's okay to share stupid stuff with them, you know! Boys you fancy don't have to think you're perfect."

Hmm. I sat back and actually replayed the last ten minutes in my head. Luke had sat and talked to me. Talked. To me! And we had enjoyed an actual, real conversation! He had showed me his phone, and said funny things, and even said I was clever!

Suddenly delighted with myself, I took an over-ambitious bite of lolly, causing the rest of it to promptly slide off the stick and into my open school bag, where it started to melt over my patched-up swimming cap. Maybe it was time to throw the swimming cap in the bin.

Paradise Regained

ON THE FOLLOWING TUESDAY, I WAS EN route to the newsagent's when Jez called my mobile and casually asked how Poppy was. If I didn't know any better, I'd say he sounded like he was missing her slightly.

"She's fine, absolutely fine," I lied airily. I rounded the corner, went into the newsagent's, and almost bumped right into Luke by the magazine rack! He looked up.

"I've got to go," I told Jez. I looked at Luke and smiled. As I'd told Poppy, even academic people are allowed to fancy exceptionally good-looking people. It is a stimulus to the brain and therefore beneficial to history homework and so on. Luke promptly picked up *What Mobile?* magazine and waved it at me. "Are you sure you don't need this?"

"No, I love my ancient, rubbish phone," I said firmly.

"I like that top, by the way."

Oh my God.

"Thanks!" I managed. I had been wearing the white halterneck with that over-the-top regularity reserved for new favorites. I didn't mention it used to be Claudia's.

Luke changed the subject. "Hope I didn't interrupt your conversation."

"It was only Jez."

Luke raised an eyebrow. "He escaped from Claudia's clutches long enough to call for help?"

I maturely suppressed any delight at this assessment of Claudia.

"I thought you liked her!" I said as lightly as possible. I mean, I'd gathered that he didn't, but I didn't really know why. I opened the nearest magazine for effect, but unfortunately it was one with scantily clad women all over it. I hastily put it down.

"Why did you think that?" said Luke.

"I saw you walking down Rosehill Road one time, and you looked—well, like a couple."

"What, we were walking down the street together?"

"Uh—yes. You were talking." I picked up *Cosmo-GIRL!* and focused intently on the cover.

"Oh—that time. With Poppy. I didn't see you," Luke said as we drifted toward the till.

"Well"—I was hiding behind a red Nissan—"I was just passing. I think you might have stopped outside here, actually." (Might have? It was still engrained in my memory.)

Luke frowned. "Yes, I remember."

I tried to arrange my expression so it looked like I didn't need to hear any more. I don't think it succeeded because Luke looked at me, then smiled slightly and continued. "She and Poppy had taken over the living room with DVDs and stuff, and these ridiculous hair flatteners—"

"Straighteners."

"Straighteners—that Claudia was attacking Poppy's hair with. So I was going to Craig's to get away from all the giggling, and then just as I was leaving, Claudia decided she had to come too because she wanted to come here—to the newsagent's. So she and Poppy ended up walking behind me and Claudia left Poppy behind and came to talk to me! I thought that was really rude, considering Poppy had invited her over, then when we got here, Poppy went in and suddenly Claudia said she would wait outside! It was so childish. I was going to leave them to it but Claudia made some comment about not feeling safe waiting for Poppy on her own, as if she'd stepped into a really dodgy area or something by leaving posh Lansdowne. So there I was waiting with her for no apparent reason. I asked why she didn't just go into the newsagent's with Poppy, since she was spending the evening with her. Then she basically told me she was only being friends with my sister in order to get close to me. I think I was supposed to be flattered! I didn't say anything to Poppy, of course. She was all caught up with Claudia, having a whale of a time. I didn't want her to be hurt. But I didn't appreciate it."

He drew breath and I realized I was holding mine.

"And she's not my type."

I managed to stop standing there like a lemon and hand the newsagent my money.

"She's just a bit—plastic or something," Luke concluded.

Like a beaker! I thought to myself.

"Like a bag?" said the newsagent.

"Pardon?" I said.

"Would you like a bag?"

"Oh—yes, please."

The newsagent handed me a flimsy blue bag and glanced at Luke, then back at me. Then he gave me a huge smile!

HOW ON EARTH COULD THIS HAVE happened? Our parents said Poppy and I could go on a week's camping holiday in Cornwall! Mum told me over dinner. She said she and Dad were treating this as a reward for doing well in my exams. Since when did they focus on my exam results? I *knew* something Very Odd was going on, because when I got back from the newsagent's my mum was on the phone to Poppy's mum! They never needed to speak on the phone! Not normal. Not normal at all.

I had gone upstairs extra-slow in the hope of hearing an informative snippet, but Mum had just been repeating "uh huh, uh huh" again and again. Honestly, how could they sit talking on the phone and not even say anything useful? They only lived a few doors away from each other.

After the trip had been announced, I looked at

Mum and Dad, puzzled. "How come you changed your mind?"

"Fresh air," said Dad succinctly. Then he spoiled the caring-parent effect somewhat by adding, "And it's half the price of that other, glossy one."

How exciting! It was a different company but it was basically the same kind of holiday as Claudia and Jo's! I headed straight over to Poppy's, only to encounter her sprinting down the road toward my house. When she saw me she burst into an on-the-spot jiggy dance, which looked like she needed the loo. "Holiday!" she squealed deafeningly, and gave me an excited hug. As I suspected, this news had totally taken her mind off Jez.

"I can't wait," I said. "Our first holiday without parents or teachers!"

"I bet there is a disco on the last night," said Poppy with relish.

"With lots of boys!"

"And Spin the Bottle!"

"That brochure says we're split into 'suitable age groups' and everything," I said. "'To foster lifelong friendships.'"

"That one Claudia's going on is fourteen to

eighteen! You know what that means? Lots of fit eighteen-year-old boys!"

"Although," I said, adopting a mock-serious expression. "You did say you had a headache the other day. It could be serious. Maybe you should stay at home."

Poppy shut up for a moment, and then burst out with, "Boys! Beaches! Nothing is keeping me away!"

I T WAS THE LAST WEEK OF TERM AND I realized it was about time I talked to Jo, since I'd been avoiding her for ages now.

"Hi," I said quickly as I sat down next to her in French on Wednesday. I observed the surrounding chaos. "Is Miss Rustford not here?"

"She's late."

I put my bag on the desk, looked down, and made an involuntarily "Hmmph!" noise at the *C loves J* freshly written onto the surface. Jo heard me. "How's Poppy?" she said candidly.

"Slightly better since, um—"

"Since shouting at Claudia?"

"Er—yes." (And since we had heard about our

group holiday. All the planning had really cheered Poppy up—especially estimating how many boys would be there.)

"And since even you shouted at Claudia, too?"

"Er—yes. Even me."

"I do think Claudia was completely out of order, you know."

I didn't know quite what to say back, having attempted diplomacy all year. It was the first time I'd heard Jo say anything negative about Claudia. But I was really curious.

"I thought—you know, I thought you got on well," I said. I would have normally stopped there, but I felt bold enough to say, "I've never been sure *why* exactly, but—"

Jo laughed. "I do like her. Of course she's not perfect. But she's okay, really."

"Well—I thought so too for a minute, but—"

"Half the time she just wants to prove to herself that she can get people to fancy her!" said Jo. "It's a nice boost. It reinforces that she's more attractive than everybody else."

"But—well—she *is*," I said. "She doesn't seem as if she needs proof."

"But you wouldn't want to be Claudia, would you?" asked Jo searchingly.

It was an odd question. I'd never thought about it before. "Well—she gets tons of freedom. It must be great."

"But—like—her parents aren't together, are they?" said Jo. "They don't seem to actually bother about her that much, just compete to give her more and more stuff. I don't think she's that secure."

"So she decides to steal someone else's boyfriend?" I probed.

"Well, Jez wasn't actually with Poppy. And it's not always that deliberate."

"What, it just happens by accident?" I said, a sharp note creeping unavoidably into my voice as I pictured Poppy crying in her room. "I mean, Jez isn't even the first, is he? There was that bloke Greg as well who dumped his girlfriend—what?"

Jo was looking at me funny. "Greg," she echoed, "hmm."

"What do you mean, 'Greg, hmm'?"

Jo winced and looked round to check Bethan was out of earshot. Miss Rustford still hadn't turned up. Fortunately Susanna Forbes was ill, so no one had dashed to the staff room about it. "Listen, don't tell anyone, but that whole Greg thing didn't quite go to plan. Claudia really liked him. They did some serious eyelash-fluttering by the sound of it, and arranged to go out that time. But he didn't show up."

"Oh no!"

"He decided he was going to stay with his girl-friend."

"But why didn't she say anything?"

"She was embarrassed—and really hurt."

I was stunned.

Jo continued. "Like when Luke didn't fall at her feet. She just felt humiliated by it. Do you remember? She just blanked anyone involved for a while, rather than deal with it. Same with Greg—she whitewashed it and moved on. Boys are her specialist subject; she doesn't like failing."

I thought back. "When Claudia told us she had dumped Greg—that was before we all went round to Jez's house."

Jo nodded. "I think so."

"So—the whole Jez thing was just Claudia trying to prove that she could have anyone she wanted, that she was still attractive?"

"Yes, that would make sense. I doubt she meant it to happen right from the start. It must have just . . . begun to feel like a good plan."

So it wasn't completely calculated, then. It did make sense. I mean, who was mean enough to befriend someone and then steal the person they fancied? Claudia had really liked Poppy, certainly by the second time, and hadn't set out to get Jez in particular—he had just been there.

I was still opening and closing my mouth in surprise when suddenly Miss Rustford swept into the room. "Sorry I'm late, girls."

I noticed she was beaming. "I was just telling the headmistress," Miss Rustford continued. "Well—I have some news."

I thought maybe school was canceled due to the surprise Claudia-is-a-human-being revelation, but Miss Rustford said, "I'm leaving at the start of the summer holidays. I'm moving to Birmingham!"

Then Bethan said, "Isn't that where Peter the coach driver is from, Miss?"

Miss Rustford actually blushed and said, "I—well, that's none of your business, Bethan!"

Bethan looked very pleased with her deduction skills.

"Miss Rustford's out of breath!" muttered Charlotte.

"Must be from all the snogging," said Sasha.

Everyone stifled gagging noises.

You know what is even more surprising than Miss Rustford having a love life? She handed out the French results, and she gave half of us A grades, including me!

A Room With a View

THE DAY BEFORE BREAKING UP FOR THE summer holidays, I discovered something Very Interesting. I had opened the bedroom window after school on Thursday because it was so hot and I could hear Mum and Mrs. Heathfield chatting in the front garden. They were trimming the hedge and I wasn't really listening. That is, until I heard Mrs. Heathfield mention my name!

". . . Holly's holiday," was all I managed to catch of the first sentence.

"Yes, we decided she could go," said Mum. There were industrious clipping noises as they both pruned and trimmed.

"I thought George had decided it was too expensive?"

"Well, that one in Spain cost a fortune, I mean, honestly—but then Elaine Taylor found a very reasonable one, in Cornwall somewhere, and we had a chat about it. She was quite keen that Poppy have a proper break this summer."

Mrs. Heathfield's response was obscured by the sound of a big bit of hedge hitting the gravel at her feet.

Mum continued. "She didn't look into it until just after the girls did their exams. Those teachers do pile on the pressure, you know, it is a *very* good school"— Mum put proper emphasis on these words—"but Holly kept going over there looking really worried, and apparently Poppy was quiet and red-eyed for weeks. And then she went really pale—got far too worked up about the results. Apparently Poppy's normally a complete hypochondriac! But she didn't mention the stress at all and Elaine got worried it could actually be serious."

I suppressed a loud snort. As if! Any tears were definitely Jez-related, and any pallor due to that sample of Hide the Red foundation.

Mum continued. "And—well—Holly does tend to stay cooped up in her room, you know. George and I would love for her to get out and about, do some cycling, or play volleyball or something. I'm sure she'd love it if only she tried. So maybe a holiday in the fresh air will get her into that kind of thing."

Urrrgghh! I nearly blew my cover with a loud snort. I knew it! Still secretly optimistic.

"So you agreed the girls should have a break?"

"Oh, can I just borrow those clippers—thanks. Yes, well—it's a funny old thing, but"—Mum lowered her voice—"I suppose I was a bit unsure whether Holly was, you know, quite old enough. I mean, she's growing up so fast, but she's still very young in some ways. . . ."

Grr.

"But then, well, I don't normally listen to Holly's conversations—"

Ha!

"—but I did accidentally overhear her chatting on the phone to Poppy the other day."

I sat bolt upright. Oh God, what? WHAT? And how come I was not in trouble? I crept silently over toward the window so I could hear better.

"Well, it changed my mind a bit. From what I could gather, some girl in their class had been boasting that she played truant for a day with some boy."

I did a silent scream. At that point there was a large

amount of falling hedge and I just heard Mum going, "Yes, I mean, you can imagine how concerned . . . but the girls knew it wasn't right! They were so disapproving! Saying it was really wrong of them. Much more mature than I had given them credit for. More grown up than Ivy at eighteen!"

I crouched by the window in disbelief. Mum thought (albeit wrongly) that I was better than Ivy at something? And then—yeeessss!—I did a little sitting-on-the-floor-by-the-window jiggy dance to celebrate. The tables had finally turned—I had listened in on my own mother! More to the point, it appeared that Claudia kindly bunking off with Jez—and Mum having eavesdropped on me—were the reasons for our holiday!

MMM. IT WAS REALLY SUNNY ON THE day we broke up for the summer holidays. I had my bedroom window wide open and there was a nice blue sky with vapor trails from planes headed from Gatwick Airport to the South of France, or Jamaica perhaps. There were birds tweeting in a summery kind of way. Mum was out at badminton and when I told her I didn't want to go along to watch, she actually said I could stay at home! What freedom. I could phone Australia on the landline, if I knew anyone who lived there.

Ha, ha. Almost forgot. In the morning Claudia looked really annoyed when Poppy loudly told Bethan we were going on holiday too. Then Jo passed me a note telling me that Jez and Claudia weren't speaking! Apparently Jez went over to Claudia's and found the boy-girl ratio of 70:30 circled in red pen on her holiday brochure! And no one did any work in French because it was a half day at school and Miss Rustford's last lesson. Poppy spent the entire morning writing me notes saying we had to watch summer-romance type films to prepare for the barbecues on the beach, swimming under waterfalls, etc.! I had to remind her that it was officially camping, and I would NOT be doing any swimming, but she clearly didn't care about the details. Finally, when the last bell went, we gave Miss Rustford a card drawn by Charlotte with a picture of Miss Rustford and Peter on a coach heading off into the sunset! Miss Rustford said she would miss us all. Us! Year Nine! She looked almost tearful for a moment, then claimed she had chalk in her eye.

So, there I was feeling all free and summery, when I heard somebody whistling outside my window. I thought it was Jamie and dashed over with a half-formed insult on my lips. But it was Luke.

Luke! Outside my house!

He looked tanned and gorgeous in jeans and a white T-shirt. He was holding a box of some kind.

"Poppy's not here," I said regretfully, leaning my hands on the windowsill.

"I know," said Luke, craning his neck to look up at me. "She's at home on the phone to Jez. It's you I wanted to see."

"Jez?" I said, thinking, "Me?"

"Yes—I know. He just phoned her. They're talking again and everything. He sounds a bit gutted that she's off on holiday. But that's not—well, the reason I came over is that I just got a new camera phone, so my old one's spare. It's a bit newer than yours—I thought you might want it?"

Did I want a mobile? Luke's mobile?

"Remind me what's it like?" I said inanely. I was still in shock that he was there, in my front garden, bits of recently trimmed hedge around his feet.

"I'll show you."

Before I could properly take in what was happening, Luke used his free hand to grab the post supporting the porch, put one foot against it and hoisted himself effortlessly up. He stood on top of the porch, level with my open window. It was incredible. Our faces were parallel and I could smell his aftershave, except this time it wasn't on his scarf. He was there with it!

Luke looked behind me at the cabin bed.

"How come you got the small room?"

"I'm planning to move into the loft room over the summer." Actually, years in the boxroom had just become worthwhile. I suddenly felt fond of it.

"Here," Luke said. He handed me the box.

I tried not to sway, faint, or die of shock. "So . . . Poppy was really okay talking to Jez?" I managed.

"She's rambling on quite happily about the holiday."

"It's brilliant that it's cheered her up."

"It's thanks to you mainly. . . ." Luke adjusted his footing. "You were really good when she was upset. I never know what to say."

I suppressed a particularly strong urge to hug him. "You shouldn't worry," I said firmly. "Girls aren't a different species, you know. Just act normally."

We were interrupted by the sound of footsteps behind us in the street as Lorraine walked past, talking at full volume into her mobile. "Well, in that case tell him to meet us in the Crown . . . hang on." She looked up momentarily at Luke standing on the porch and then continued, "No, don't worry. It's that weird girl— that one who's always staring out of her window— having a *Romeo and Juliet* moment. Don't ask me."

Luke appeared unfazed. He turned back, said "May I?" and got the mobile out of the box I was holding. "It's a good phone."

"Thanks!" I said, thinking, *Romeo and Juliet* balcony scene! This clearly counted as fulfillment of a Favorite Fantasy, even if Luke was holding a phone rather than a rose.

"The menu works like this, and this is the text message option on this screen here. You might want to disable that bit actually."

"Is it broken?"

"No, it works—it just occurred to me that, well, you need to talk more, rather than write."

"Oh!"

"Well," said Luke, looking into my eyes. "I guess . . . I'll see you when you get back from your holiday?"

"Okay."

"Have fun."

"Will do," I said dazedly.

Just as I was thinking, Don't hug him, don't hug him, he moved closer and murmured, "*Romeo and Juliet*, eh?"

That was when it happened. He kissed me.

Kissed me! Just quickly, but on the lips! With a meaningful, right-in-the-eyes look to accompany it afterward! Then he turned, jumped down off the porch, and headed back toward his house! It was amazing. Ten thousand glitterballs spinning around the sun could not have made life as sparkly. I felt dizzy, in much the same way as when I accidentally skied down that mountain. But better.

I spent a while staring out of the window at the clear blue sky. I would have to update my Who-Likes-Who chart. But that could wait. For the moment I was going to key my friends' numbers into my new phone, and enjoy the sense of promise in the summer air.

The adorable, delicious—
and très stylish—adventures of
Imogene are delighting readers
around the globe.
Don't miss these darling
new favorites!

A Girl Like Moi

Project Paris

by Lisa Barham

From Simon Pulse
Published by Simon & Schuster